THE BEE-MAN OF ORN

AND

OTHER FANCIFUL TALES

BY

FRANK R. STOCKTON

NEW YORK

CHARLES SCRIBNER'S SONS

1887

CONTENTS.

THE BEE-MAN OF ORN.

IN the ancient country of Orn, there lived an old
man who was called the Bee-man, because his whole
time was spent in the company of bees. He lived in a
small hut, which was nothing more than an immense
bee-hive, for these little creatures had built their honey-
combs in every corner of the one room it contained, on
the shelves, under the little table, all about the rough
bench on which the old man sat, and even about the
head-board and along the sides of his low bed. All
day the air of the room was thick with buzzing insects,
but this did not interfere in any way with the old Bee-
man, who walked in among them, ate his meals, and
went to sleep, without the slightest fear of being
stung. He had lived with the bees so long, they had
become so accustomed to him, and his skin was so
tough and hard, that the bees no more thought of
stinging him than they would of stinging a tree or
a stone. A swarm of bees had made their hive in a
pocket of his old leathern doublet; and when he put
on this coat to take one of his long walks in the forest
in search of wild bees' nests, he was very glad to have
this hive with him, for, if he did not find any wild

1

honey, he would put his hand in his pocket and take out a piece of a comb for a luncheon. The bees in his pocket worked very industriously, and he was always certain of having something to eat with him wherever he went. He lived principally upon honey; and when he needed bread or meat, he carried some fine combs to a village not far away and bartered them for other food. He was ugly, untidy, shrivelled, and brown. He was poor, and the bees seemed to be his only friends. But, for all that, he was happy and contented; he had all the honey he wanted, and his bees, whom he considered the best company in the world, were as friendly and sociable as they could be, and seemed to increase in number every day.

One day, there stopped at the hut of the Bee-man a Junior Sorcerer. This young person, who was a student of magic, necromancy, and the kindred arts, was much interested in the Bee-man, whom he had frequently noticed in his wanderings, and he considered him an admirable subject for study. He had got a great deal of useful practice by endeavoring to find out, by the various rules and laws of sorcery, exactly why the old Bee-man did not happen to be something that he was not, and why he was what he happened to be. He had studied a long time at this matter, and had found out something.

"Do you know," he said, when the Bee-man came out of his hut, "that you have been transformed?"

"What do you mean by that?" said the other, much surprised.

"You have surely heard of animals and human

beings who have been magically transformed into different kinds of creatures?"

"Yes, I have heard of these things," said the Bee-man; " but what have I been transformed from?"

"That is more than I know," said the Junior Sorcerer. "But one thing is certain — you ought to be changed back. If you will find out what you have been transformed from, I will see that you are made all right again. Nothing would please me better than to attend to such a case."

And, having a great many things to study and investigate, the Junior Sorcerer went his way.

This information greatly disturbed the mind of the Bee-man. If he had been changed from something else, he ought to be that other thing, whatever it was. He ran after the young man, and overtook him.

"If you know, kind sir," he said, "that I have been transformed, you surely are able to tell me what it is that I was."

"No," said the Junior Sorcerer, " my studies have not proceeded far enough for that. When I become a senior I can tell you all about it. But, in the meantime, it will be well for you to try to discover for yourself your original form, and when you have done that, I will get some of the learned masters of my art to restore you to it. It will be easy enough to do that, but you could not expect them to take the time and trouble to find out what it was."

And, with these words, he hurried away, and was soon lost to view.

Greatly disquieted, the Bee-man retraced his steps,

and went to his hut. Never before had he heard any thing which had so troubled him.

"I wonder what I was transformed from?" he thought, seating himself on his rough bench. "Could it have been a giant, or a powerful prince, or some gorgeous being whom the magicians or the fairies wished to punish? It may be that I was a dog or a horse, or perhaps a fiery dragon or a horrid snake. I hope it was not one of these. But, whatever it was, every one has certainly a right to his original form, and I am resolved to find out mine. I will start early to-morrow morning, and I am sorry now that I have not more pockets to my old doublet, so that I might carry more bees and more honey for my journey."

He spent the rest of the day in making a hive of twigs and straw, and, having transferred to this a number of honey-combs and a colony of bees which had just swarmed, he rose before sunrise the next day, and having put on his leathern doublet, and having bound his new hive to his back, he set forth on his quest; the bees who were to accompany him buzzing around him like a cloud.

As the Bee-man passed through the little village the people greatly wondered at his queer appearance, with the hive upon his back. "The Bee-man is going on a long expedition this time," they said; but no one imagined the strange business on which he was bent. About noon he sat down under a tree, near a beautiful meadow covered with blossoms, and ate a little honey. Then he untied his hive and stretched himself out on the grass to rest. As he gazed upon his bees hovering about him, some going out to the blossoms in the sunshine, and some returning laden with the sweet pollen, he said to himself, "They know just what they have to do, and they do it; but alas for me! I know not what I may have to do. And yet, whatever it may be, I am determined to do it. In some way or other I will find out what was my original form, and then I will have myself changed back to it."

And now the thought came to him that perhaps his original form might have been something very disagreeable, or even horrid.

"But it does not matter," he said sturdily. "Whatever I was that shall I be again. It is not right for any one to retain a form which does not properly belong to him. I have no doubt I shall discover my original form in the same way that I find the trees in which the wild bees hive. When I first catch sight of a bee-tree I am drawn towards it, I know not how. Something says to me: 'That is what you are looking for.' In the same way I believe that I shall find my original form. When I see it, I shall be drawn towards it. Something will say to me: 'That is it.'"

When the Bee-man was rested he started off again, and in about an hour he entered a fair domain. Around him were beautiful lawns, grand trees, and lovely gardens; while at a little distance stood the stately palace of the Lord of the Domain. Richly dressed people were walking about or sitting in the shade of the trees and arbors; splendidly caparisoned horses were waiting for their riders; and everywhere were seen signs of opulence and gayety.

" I think," said the Bee-man to himself, " that I should like to stop here for a time. If it should happen that I was originally like any of these happy creatures it would please me much."

He untied his hive, and hid it behind some bushes, and taking off his old doublet, laid that beside it. It would not do to have his bees flying about him if he wished to go among the inhabitants of this fair domain.

For two days the Bee-man wandered about the palace and its grounds, avoiding notice as much as possible, but looking at every thing. He saw handsome men and lovely ladies; the finest horses, dogs, and cattle that were ever known; beautiful birds in cages, and fishes in crystal globes, and it seemed to him that the best of all living things were here collected.

At the close of the second day, the Bee-man said to himself: " There is one being here toward whom I feel very much drawn, and that is the Lord of the Domain. I cannot feel certain that I was once like him, but it would be a very fine thing if it were so; and it seems impossible for me to be drawn toward any other being in the domain when I look upon him, so handsome, rich, and powerful. But I must observe him more closely, and feel more sure of the matter, before applying to the sorcerers to change me back into a lord of a fair domain."

The next morning, the Bee-man saw the Lord of the Domain walking in his gardens. He slipped along the shady paths, and followed him so as to observe him closely, and find out if he were really drawn toward this noble and handsome being. The Lord of the Domain walked on for some time, not noticing that the Bee-man was behind him. But suddenly turning, he saw the little old man.

"What are you doing here, you vile beggar?" he cried; and he gave him a kick that sent him into some bushes that grew by the side of the path.

The Bee-man scrambled to his feet, and ran as fast as he could to the place where he had hidden his hive and his old doublet.

"If I am certain of any thing," he thought, "it is that I was never a person who would kick a poor old man. I will leave this place. I was transformed from nothing that I see here."

He now travelled for a day or two longer, and then he came to a great black mountain, near the bottom of which was an opening like the mouth of a cave.

This mountain he had heard was filled with caverns and under-ground passages, which were the abodes of dragons, evil spirits, horrid creatures of all kinds.

"Ah me!" said the Bee-man with a sigh, "I suppose I ought to visit this place. If I am going to do this thing properly, I should look on all sides of the subject, and I may have been one of those horrid creatures myself."

Thereupon he went to the mountain, and as he approached the opening of the passage which led into its inmost recesses he saw, sitting upon the ground, and leaning his back against a tree, a Languid Youth.

"Good-day," said this individual when he saw the Bee-man. "Are you going inside?"

"Yes," said the Bee-man, " that is what I intend to do."

" Then," said the Languid Youth, slowly rising to his feet, " I think I will go with you. I was told that if I went in there I should get my energies toned up, and they need it very much; but I did not feel equal to entering by myself, and I thought I would wait until some one came along. I am very glad to see you, and we will go in together."

So the two went into the cave, and they had proceeded but a short distance when they met a very little creature, whom it was easy to recognize as a Very Imp. He was about two feet high, and resembled in color a freshly polished pair of boots. He was extremely lively and active, and came bounding toward them.

" What did you two people come here for?" he asked.

" I came," said the Languid Youth, " to have my energies toned up."

" You have come to the right place," said the Very Imp. " We will tone you up. And what does that old Bee-man want? "

" He has been transformed from something, and wants to find out what it is. He thinks he may have been one of the things in here."

"I should not wonder if that were so," said the Very Imp, rolling his head on one side, and eying the Bee-man with a critical gaze.

" All right," said the Very Imp ; " he can go around, and pick out his previous existence. We have here all sorts of vile creepers, crawlers, hissers, and snorters. I suppose he thinks any thing will be better than a Bee-man."

"It is not because I want to be better than I am," said the Bee-man, "that I started out on this search. I have simply an honest desire to become what I originally was."

"Oh! that is it, is it?" said the other. "There is an idiotic moon-calf here with a clam head, which must be just like what you used to be."

"Nonsense," said the Bee-man. "You have not the least idea what an honest purpose is. I shall go about, and see for myself."

"Go ahead," said the Very Imp, "and I will attend to this fellow who wants to be toned up." So saying he joined the Languid Youth.

"Look here," said that individual, regarding him with interest, "do you black and shine yourself every morning?"

"No," said the other, "it is water-proof varnish. You want to be invigorated, don't you? Well, I will tell you a splendid way to begin. You see that Bee-man has put down his hive and his coat with the bees in it. Just wait till he gets out of sight, and then catch a lot of those bees, and squeeze them flat. If you spread them on a sticky rag, and make a plaster, and put it on the small of your back, it will invigorate you like every thing, especially if some of the bees are not quite dead."

"Yes," said the Languid Youth, looking at him with his mild eyes, "but if I had energy enough to catch a bee I would be satisfied. Suppose you catch a lot for me."

"The subject is changed," said the Very Imp. "We are now about to visit the spacious chamber of the King of the Snap-dragons."

"That is a flower," said the Languid Youth.

"You will find him a gay old blossom," said the other. "When he has chased you round his room, and has blown sparks at you, and has snorted and howled, and cracked his tail, and snapped his jaws like a pair of anvils, your energies will be toned up higher than ever before in your life."

"No doubt of it," said the Languid Youth; "but I think I will begin with something a little milder."

"Well then," said other, "there is a flat-tailed Demon of the Gorge in here. He is generally asleep, and, if you say so, you can slip into the farthest corner of his cave, and I'll solder his tail to the opposite wall. Then he will rage and roar, but he can't get at you, for he does n't reach all the way across his cave; I have measured him. It will tone you up wonderfully to sit there and watch him."

"Very likely," said the Languid Youth; "but I would rather stay outside and let you go up in the corner. The performance in that way will be more interesting to me."

"You are dreadfully hard to please," said the Very Imp. "I have offered them to you loose, and I have offered them fastened to a wall, and now the best thing I can do is to give you a chance at one of them that can't move at all. It is the Ghastly Griffin and is enchanted. He can't stir so much as the tip of his whiskers for a thousand years. You can go to his cave and examine him just as if he were stuffed, and then you can sit on his back and think how it would be if you should live to be a thousand years old, and he should wake up while you are sitting there. It would be easy to imagine a lot of horrible things he would do to you when you look at his open mouth with its awful fangs, his dreadful claws, and his horrible wings all covered with spikes.''

'' I think that might suit me,'' said the Languid Youth. '' I would much rather imagine the exercises of these monsters than to see them really going on.''

'' Come on, then,'' said the Very Imp, and he led the way to the cave of the Ghastly Griffin.

The Bee-man went by himself through a great part of the mountain, and looked into many of its gloomy caves and recesses, recoiling in horror from most of the dreadful monsters who met his eyes. While he was wandering about, an awful roar was heard resounding through the passages of the mountain, and soon there came flapping along an enormous dragon, with body black as night, and wings and tail of fiery red. In his great fore-claws he bore a little baby.

'' Horrible ! '' exclaimed the Bee-man. '' He is taking that little creature to his cave to devour it.''

He saw the dragon enter a cave not far away, and following looked in. The dragon was crouched upon the ground with the little baby lying before him. It did not seem to be hurt, but was frightened and crying. The monster was looking upon it with delight, as if he intended to make a dainty meal of it as soon as his appetite should be a little stronger.

" It is too bad ! " thought the Bee-man. " Somebody ought to do something." And turning around, he ran away as fast as he could.

He ran through various passages until he came to the spot where he had left his bee-hive. Picking it up, he hurried back, carrying the hive in his two hands before him. When he reached the cave of the dragon, he looked in and saw the monster still crouched over the weeping child. Without a moment's hesitation, the Bee-man rushed into the cave and threw his hive straight into the face of the dragon. The bees, enraged by the shock, rushed out in an angry crowd and immediately fell upon the head, mouth, eyes, and nose of the dragon. The great monster, astounded by this sudden attack, and driven almost wild by the numberless stings of the bees, sprang back to the farthest portion of his cave, still followed by his relentless enemies, at whom he flapped wildly with his great wings and struck with his paws. While the dragon was thus engaged with the bees, the Bee-man rushed forward, and, seizing the child, he hurried away. He did not stop to pick up his doublet, but kept on until he reached the entrance of the caves. There he saw the Very Imp hopping along on one leg, and rubbing his back and shoulders with his hands, and stopped to inquire what was the matter, and what had become of the Languid Youth.

" He is no kind of a fellow," said the Very Imp. " He disappointed me dreadfully. I took him up to

the Ghastly Griffin, and told him the thing was enchanted, and that he might sit on its back and think
about what it could do if it was awake; and when
he came near it the wretched creature opened its eyes,
and raised its head, and then you ought to have seen
how mad that simpleton was. He made a dash at me
and seized me by the ears; he kicked and beat me
till I can scarcely move."

"His energies must have been toned up a good
deal," said the Bee-man.

"Toned up! I should say so!" cried the other. "I
raised a howl, and a Scissor-jawed Clipper came out
of his hole, and got after him; but that lazy fool ran
so fast that he could not be caught."

The Bee-man now ran on and soon overtook the
Languid Youth.

"You need not be in a hurry now," said the latter,
"for the rules of this institution don't allow the
creatures inside to come out of this opening, or to hang
around it. If they did, they would frighten away
visitors. They go in and out of holes in the upper
part of the mountain."

The two proceeded on their way.

"What are you going to do with that baby?" said
the Languid Youth.

"I shall carry it along with me," said the Bee-man,
"as I go on with my search, and perhaps I may find
its mother. If I do not, I shall give it to somebody
in that little village yonder. Any thing would be better than leaving it to be devoured by that horrid
dragon."

" Let me carry it. I feel quite strong enough now to carry a baby."

" Thank you," said the Bee-man, " but I can take it myself. I like to carry something, and I have now neither my hive nor my doublet."

" It is very well that you had to leave them behind," said the Youth, " for the bees would have stung the baby."

" My bees never sting babies," said the other.

" They probably never had a chance," remarked his companion.

They soon entered the village, and after walking a short distance the youth exclaimed : " Do you see that woman over there sitting at the door of her house? She has beautiful hair and she is tearing it all to pieces. She should not be allowed to do that."

" No," said the Bee-man. " Her friends should tie her hands."

" Perhaps she is the mother of this child," said the Youth, " and if you give it to her she will no longer think of tearing her hair."

" But," said the Bee-man, " you don't really think this is her child?"

" Suppose you go over and see," said the other.

The Bee-man hesitated a moment, and then he walked toward the woman. Hearing him coming, she raised her head, and when she saw the child she rushed towards it, snatched it into her arms, and screaming with joy she covered it with kisses. Then with happy tears she begged to know the story of the rescue of her child, whom she never expected to see again ; and she loaded the Bee-man with thanks and blessings. The friends and neighbors gathered around and there was great rejoicing. The mother urged the Bee-man and the Youth to stay with her, and rest and refresh themselves, which they were glad to do as they were tired and hungry.

They remained at the cottage all night, and in the afternoon of the next day the Bee-man said to the Youth : " It may seem an odd thing to you, but never in all my life have I felt myself drawn towards any living being as I am drawn towards this baby. Therefore I believe that I have been transformed from a baby."

"Good!" cried the Youth. "It is my opinion that you have hit the truth. And now would you like to be changed back to your original form?"

" Indeed I would! " said the Bee-man, " I have the strongest yearning to be what I originally was."

The Youth, who had now lost every trace of languid feeling, took a great interest in the matter, and early the next morning started off to inform the Junior Sorcerer that the Bee-man had discovered what he had been transformed from, and desired to be changed back to it.

The Junior Sorcerer and his learned Masters were filled with enthusiasm when they heard this report, and they at once set out for the mother's cottage. And there by magic arts the Bee-man was changed back into a baby. The mother was so grateful for what the Bee-man had done for her that she agreed to take charge of this baby, and to bring it up as her own.

" It will be a grand thing for him," said the Junior Sorcerer, " and I am glad that I studied his case. He will now have a fresh start in life, and will have a chance to become something better than a miserable old man living in a wretched hut with no friends or companions but buzzing bees."

The Junior Sorcerer and his Masters then returned to their homes, happy in the success of their great performance ; and the Youth went back to his home anxious to begin a life of activity and energy.

Years and years afterward, when the Junior Sorcerer had become a Senior and was very old indeed, he passed through the country of Orn, and noticed a small hut about which swarms of bees were flying. He approached it, and looking in at the door he saw an old man in a leathern doublet, sitting at a table, eating honey. By his magic art he knew this was the baby which had been transformed from the Bee-man.

" Upon my word !" exclaimed the Sorcerer, " He has grown into the same thing again ! "

THE GRIFFIN AND THE MINOR CANON.

O VER the great door of an old, old church which stood in a quiet town of a far-away land there was carved in stone the figure of a large griffin. The old-time sculptor had done his work with great care, but the image he had made was not a pleasant one to look at. It had a large head, with enormous open mouth and savage teeth; from its back arose great wings, armed with sharp hooks and prongs; it had stout legs in front, with projecting claws; but there were no legs behind, — the body running out into a long and powerful tail, finished off at the end with a barbed point. This tail was coiled up under him, the end sticking up just back of his wings.

The sculptor, or the people who had ordered this stone figure, had evidently been very much pleased with it, for little copies of it, also in stone, had been placed here and there along the sides of the church, not very far from the ground, so that people could easily look at them, and ponder on their curious forms. There were a great many other sculptures on the outside of this church, — saints, martyrs, grotesque heads of men, beasts, and birds, as well as those of other creatures which cannot be named, because nobody knows exactly what they were; but none were so curious and interesting as the great griffin over the door, and the little griffins on the sides of the church.

A long, long distance from the town, in the midst of dreadful wilds scarcely known to man, there dwelt the Griffin whose image had been put up over the church-door. In some way or other, the old-time sculptor had seen him, and afterward, to the best of his memory, had copied his figure in stone. The Griffin had never known this, until, hundreds of years afterward, he heard from a bird, from a wild animal, or in some manner which it is not now easy to find out, that there was a likeness of him on the old church in the distant town. Now, this Griffin had no idea how he looked. He had never seen a mirror, and the streams where he lived were so turbulent and violent that a quiet piece of water, which would reflect the image of any thing looking into it, could not be found. Being, as far as could be ascertained, the very last of his race, he had never seen another griffin. Therefore it was, that, when he heard of this stone image of himself, he became very anxious to know what he looked like, and at last he determined to go to the old church, and see for himself what manner of being he was. So he started off from the dreadful wilds, and flew on and on until he came to the countries inhabited by men, where his appearance in the air created great consternation; but he alighted nowhere, keeping up a steady flight until he reached the suburbs of the town which had his image on its church. Here, late in the afternoon, he alighted in a green meadow by the side of a brook, and stretched himself on the grass to rest. His great wings were tired, for he had not made such a long flight in a century, or more.

The news of his coming spread quickly over the town, and the people, frightened nearly out of their wits by the arrival of so extraordinary a visitor, fled into their houses, and shut themselves up. The Griffin called loudly for some one to come to him, but the more he called, the more afraid the people were to show themselves. At length he saw two laborers hurrying to their homes through the fields, and in a terrible voice he commanded them to stop. Not daring to disobey, the men stood, trembling.

"What is the matter with you all?" cried the Griffin. "Is there not a man in your town who is brave enough to speak to me?"

"I think," said one of the laborers, his voice shaking so that his words could hardly be understood, "that — perhaps — the Minor Canon — would come."

"Go, call him, then!" said the Griffin; "I want to see him."

The Minor Canon, who filled a subordinate position in the old church, had just finished the afternoon services, and was coming out of a side door, with three aged women who had formed the week-day congregation. He was a young man of a kind disposition, and very anxious to do good to the people of the town. Apart from his duties in the church, where he conducted services every week-day, he visited the sick and the poor, counselled and assisted persons who were

in trouble, and taught a school composed entirely of
the bad children in the town with whom nobody else
would have any thing to do. Whenever the people
wanted something difficult done for them, they always
went to the Minor Canon. Thus it was that the
laborer thought of the young priest when he found that
some one must come and speak to the Griffin.

The Minor Canon had not heard of the strange
event, which was known to the whole town except
himself and the three old women, and when he was
informed of it, and was told that the Griffin had asked
to see him, he was greatly amazed, and frightened.

"Me!" he exclaimed. "He has never heard of
me! What should he want with *me?*"

"Oh! you must go instantly!" cried the two men.
"He is very angry now because he has been kept waiting so long; and nobody knows what may happen if
you don't hurry to him."

The poor Minor Canon would rather have had his
hand cut off than go out to meet an angry griffin; but
he felt that it was his duty to go, for it would be a
woful thing if injury should come to the people of the
town because he was not brave enough to obey the
summons of the Griffin. So, pale and frightened, he
started off.

"Well," said the Griffin, as soon as the young man
came near, "I am glad to see that there is some one
who has the courage to come to me."

The Minor Canon did not feel very courageous, but
he bowed his head.

"Is this the town," said the Griffin, "where there

is a church with a likeness of myself over one of the doors?''

The Minor Canon looked at the frightful creature before him and saw that it was, without doubt, exactly like the stone image on the church. '' Yes,'' he said, '' you are right.''

'' Well, then,'' said the Griffin, '' will you take me to it? I wish very much to see it.''

The Minor Canon instantly thought that if the Griffin entered the town without the people knowing what he came for, some of them would probably be frightened to death, and so he sought to gain time to prepare their minds.

'' It is growing dark, now,'' he said, very much afraid, as he spoke, that his words might enrage the Griffin, '' and objects on the front of the church can not be seen clearly. It will be better to wait until morning, if you wish to get a good view of the stone image of yourself.''

'' That will suit me very well,'' said the Griffin. '' I see you are a man of good sense. I am tired, and I will take a nap here on this soft grass, while I cool my tail in the little stream that runs near me. The end of my tail gets red-hot when I am angry or excited, and it is quite warm now. So you may go, but be sure and come early to-morrow morning, and show me the way to the church.

The Minor Canon was glad enough to take his leave, and hurried into the town. In front of the church he found a great many people assembled to hear his report of his interview with the Griffin. When they found that he had not come to spread ruin and devastation, but simply to see his stony likeness on the church, they showed neither relief nor gratification, but began to upbraid the Minor Canon for consenting to conduct the creature into the town.

" What could I do? " cried the young man. " If I should not bring him he would come himself and, perhaps, end by setting fire to the town with his red-hot tail."

Still the people were not satisfied, and a great many plans were proposed to prevent the Griffin from coming into the town. Some elderly persons urged that the young men should go out and kill him; but the young men scoffed at such a ridiculous idea. Then some one said that it would be a good thing to destroy the stone image so that the Griffin would have no excuse for entering the town; and this proposal was received with such favor that many of the people ran for hammers, chisels, and crowbars, with which to tear down and break up the stone griffin. But the Minor Canon resisted this plan with all the strength of his mind and body. He assured the people that this action would enrage the Griffin beyond measure, for it would be impossible to conceal from him that his image had been destroyed during the night. But the people were so determined to break up the stone griffin that the Minor Canon saw that there was nothing for him to do but to stay there and protect it. All night he walked up and down in front of the church-door, keeping away the men who brought ladders, by which they might mount to the great stone griffin, and knock it to pieces with their hammers and crowbars. After many hours the people were obliged to give up their attempts, and went home to sleep; but the Minor Canon remained at his post till early morning, and then he hurried away to the field where he had left the Griffin.

The monster had just awakened, and rising to his fore-legs and shaking himself, he said that he was ready to go into the town. The Minor Canon, therefore, walked back, the Griffin flying slowly through the air, at a short distance above the head of his guide. Not a person was to be seen in the streets, and they proceeded directly to the front of the church, where the Minor Canon pointed out the stone griffin.

The real Griffin settled down in the little square before the church and gazed earnestly at his sculptured likeness. For a long time he looked at it. First he put his head on one side, and then he put it on the other; then he shut his right eye and gazed with his left, after which he shut his left eye and gazed with his right. Then he moved a little to one side and looked at the image, then he moved the other way. After a while he said to the Minor Canon, who had been standing by all this time:

"It is, it must be, an excellent likeness! That breadth between the eyes, that expansive forehead, those massive jaws! I feel that it must resemble me. If there is any fault to find with it, it is that the neck seems a little stiff. But that is nothing. It is an admirable likeness, — admirable!"

The Griffin sat looking at his image all the morning

and all the afternoon. The Minor Canon had been afraid to go away and leave him, and had hoped all through the day that he would soon be satisfied with his inspection and fly away home. But by evening the poor young man was utterly exhausted, and felt that he must eat and sleep. He frankly admitted this fact to the Griffin, and asked him if he would not like something to eat. He said this because he felt obliged in politeness to do so, but as soon as he had spoken the words, he was seized with dread lest the monster should demand half a dozen babies, or some tempting repast of that kind.

"Oh, no," said the Griffin, "I never eat between the equinoxes. At the vernal and at the autumnal equinox I take a good meal, and that lasts me for half a year. I am extremely regular in my habits, and do not think it healthful to eat at odd times. But if you need food, go and get it, and I will return to the soft grass where I slept last night and take another nap."

The next day the Griffin came again to the little square before the church, and remained there until evening, steadfastly regarding the stone griffin over the door. The Minor Canon came once or twice to look at him, and the Griffin seemed very glad to see him; but the young clergyman could not stay as he had done before, for he had many duties to perform. Nobody went to the church, but the people came to the Minor Canon's house, and anxiously asked him how long the Griffin was going to stay.

"I do not know," he answered, "but I think he

will soon be satisfied with regarding his stone likeness, and then he will go away."

But the Griffin did not go away. Morning after morning he came to the church, but after a time he did not stay there all day. He seemed to have taken a great fancy to the Minor Canon, and followed him about as he pursued his various avocations. He would wait for him at the side door of the church, for the Minor Canon held services every day, morning and evening, though nobody came now. "If any one should come," he said to himself, "I must be found at my post." When the young man came out, the Griffin would accompany him in his visits to the sick and the poor, and would often look into the windows of the school-house where the Minor Canon was teaching his unruly scholars. All the other schools were closed, but the parents of the Minor Canon's scholars forced them to go to school, because they were so bad they could not endure them all day at home, — griffin or no griffin. But it must be said they generally behaved very well when that great monster sat up on his tail and looked in at the school-room window.

When it was perceived that the Griffin showed no sign of going away, all the people who were able to do so left the town. The canons and the higher officers of the church had fled away during the first day of the Griffin's visit, leaving behind only the Minor Canon and some of the men who opened the doors and swept the church. All the citizens who could afford it shut up their houses and travelled to distant parts, and only the working people and the poor were left behind. After some days these ventured to go about and attend to their business, for if they did not work they would starve. They were getting a little used to seeing the Griffin, and having been told that he did not eat between equinoxes, they did not feel so much afraid of him as before.

Day by day the Griffin became more and more attached to the Minor Canon. He kept near him a great part of the time, and often spent the night in front of the little house where the young clergyman lived alone. This strange companionship was often burdensome to the Minor Canon; but, on the other hand, he could not deny that he derived a great deal of benefit and instruction from it. The Griffin had lived for hundreds of years, and had seen much; and he told the Minor Canon many wonderful things.

"It is like reading an old book," said the young clergyman to himself; "but how many books I would have had to read before I would have found out what the Griffin has told me about the earth, the air, the water, about minerals, and metals, and growing things, and all the wonders of the world!"

Thus the summer went on, and drew toward its close. And now the people of the town began to be very much troubled again.

"It will not be long," they said, "before the autumnal equinox is here, and then that monster will want to eat. He will be dreadfully hungry, for he has taken so much exercise since his last meal. He will devour our children. Without doubt, he will eat them all. What is to be done?"

To this question no one could give an answer, but all agreed that the Griffin must not be allowed to remain until the approaching equinox. After talking over the matter a great deal, a crowd of the people went to the Minor Canon, at a time when the Griffin was not with him.

"It is all your fault," they said, "that that monster is among us. You brought him here, and you ought to see that he goes away. It is only on your account that he stays here at all, for, although he visits his image every day, he is with you the greater part of the time. If you were not here, he would not stay. It is your duty to go away and then he will follow you, and we shall be free from the dreadful danger which hangs over us."

"Go away!" cried the Minor Canon, greatly grieved at being spoken to in such a way. "Where shall I go? If I go to some other town, shall I not take this trouble there? Have I a right to do that?"

"No," said the people, "you must not go to any other town. There is no town far enough away. You must go to the dreadful wilds where the Griffin lives; and then he will follow you and stay there."

They did not say whether or not they expected the Minor Canon to stay there also, and he did not ask them any thing about it. He bowed his head, and went into his house, to think. The more he thought, the more clear it became to his mind that it was his duty to go away, and thus free the town from the presence of the Griffin.

That evening he packed a leathern bag full of bread

and meat, and early the next morning he set out on his journey to the dreadful wilds. It was a long, weary, and doleful journey, especially after he had gone beyond the habitations of men, but the Minor Canon kept on bravely, and never faltered. The way was longer than he had expected, and his provisions soon grew so scanty that he was obliged to eat but a little every day, but he kept up his courage, and pressed on, and, after many days of toilsome travel, he reached the dreadful wilds.

When the Griffin found that the Minor Canon had left the town he seemed sorry, but showed no disposition to go and look for him. After a few days had passed, he became much annoyed, and asked some of the people where the Minor Canon had gone. But, although the citizens had been so anxious that the young clergyman should go to the dreadful wilds, thinking that the Griffin would immediately follow him, they were now afraid to mention the Minor Canon's destination, for the monster seemed angry already, and, if he should suspect their trick he would, doubtless, become very much enraged. So every one said he did not know, and the Griffin wandered about disconsolate. One morning he looked into the Minor Canon's school-house, which was always empty now, and thought that it was a shame that every thing should suffer on account of the young man's absence.

"It does not matter so much about the church," he said, "for nobody went there; but it is a pity about the school. I think I will teach it myself until he returns."

It was the hour for opening the school, and the Griffin went inside and pulled the rope which rang the school-bell. Some of the children who heard the bell ran in to see what was the matter, supposing it to be a joke of one of their companions; but when they saw the Griffin they stood astonished, and scared.

"Go tell the other scholars," said the monster, "that school is about to open, and that if they are not all here in ten minutes, I shall come after them."

In seven minutes every scholar was in place.

Never was seen such an orderly school. Not a boy or girl moved, or uttered a whisper. The Griffin climbed into the master's seat, his wide wings spread on each side of him, because he could not lean back in his chair while they stuck out behind, and his great tail coiled around, in front of the desk, the barbed end sticking up, ready to tap any boy or girl who might misbehave. The Griffin now addressed the scholars, telling them that he intended to teach them while their master was away. In speaking he endeavored to imitate, as far as possible, the mild and gentle tones of the Minor Canon, but it must be admitted that in this he was not very successful. He had paid a good deal of attention to the studies of the school, and he determined not to attempt to teach them any thing new, but to review them in what they had been studying; so he called up the various classes, and questioned them upon their previous lessons. The children racked their brains to remember what they had learned. They were so afraid of the Griffin's displeasure that they recited as they had never recited before. One of the boys, far down in his class, answered so well that the Griffin was astonished.

"I should think you would be at the head," said he. "I am sure you have never been in the habit of reciting so well. Why is this?"

"Because I did not choose to take the trouble," said the boy, trembling in his boots. He felt obliged to speak the truth, for all the children thought that the great eyes of the Griffin could see right through them, and that he would know when they told a falsehood.

"You ought to be ashamed of yourself," said the Griffin. "Go down to the very tail of the class, and if you are not at the head in two days, I shall know the reason why."

The next afternoon this boy was number one.

It was astonishing how much these children now learned of what they had been studying. It was as if they had been educated over again. The Griffin used no severity toward them, but there was a look about him which made them unwilling to go to bed until they were sure they knew their lessons for the next day.

The Griffin now thought that he ought to visit the sick and the poor; and he began to go about the town for this purpose. The effect upon the sick was miraculous. All, except those who were very ill indeed, jumped from their beds when they heard he was coming, and declared themselves quite well. To those who could not get up, he gave herbs and roots, which none of them had ever before thought of as medicines, but which the Griffin had seen used in various parts of the world; and most of them recovered. But, for all that, they afterward said that no matter what happened to them, they hoped that they should never again have such a doctor coming to their bed-sides, feeling their pulses and looking at their tongues.

As for the poor, they seemed to have utterly disappeared. All those who had depended upon charity for their daily bread were now at work in some way or other; many of them offering to do odd jobs for their neighbors just for the sake of their meals, — a thing which before had been seldom heard of in the town. The Griffin could find no one who needed his assistance.

The summer had now passed, and the autumnal equinox was rapidly approaching. The citizens were in a state of great alarm and anxiety. The Griffin showed no signs of going away, but seemed to have settled himself permanently among them. In a short time, the day for his semi-annual meal would arrive, and then what would happen? The monster would certainly be very hungry, and would devour all their children.

Now they greatly regretted and lamented that they had sent away the Minor Canon; he was the only one on whom they could have depended in this trouble, for he could talk freely with the Griffin, and so find out what could be done. But it would not do to be inactive. Some step must be taken immediately. A meeting of the citizens was called, and two old men were appointed to go and talk to the Griffin. They were instructed to offer to prepare a splendid dinner for him on equinox day, — one which would entirely satisfy his hunger. They would offer him the fattest mutton, the most tender beef, fish, and game of various sorts, and any thing of the kind that he might fancy. If none of these suited, they were to mention that there was an orphan asylum in the next town.

"Any thing would be better," said the citizens, "than to have our dear children devoured."

The old men went to the Griffin, but their propositions were not received with favor.

"From what I have seen of the people of this town," said the monster, "I do not think I could relish any thing which was prepared by them. They appear to be all cowards, and, therefore, mean and selfish. As for eating one of them, old or young, I could not think of it for a moment. In fact, there was only one creature in the whole place for whom I could have had any appetite, and that is the Minor Canon, who has gone away. He was brave, and good, and honest, and I think I should have relished him."

"Ah!" said one of the old men very politely, "in that case I wish we had not sent him to the dreadful wilds!"

"What!" cried the Griffin. "What do you mean? Explain instantly what you are talking about!"

The old man, terribly frightened at what he had said, was obliged to tell how the Minor Canon had been sent away by the people, in the hope that the Griffin might be induced to follow him.

When the monster heard this, he became furiously angry. He dashed away from the old men and, spreading his wings, flew backward and forward over the town. He was so much excited that his tail became red-hot, and glowed like a meteor against the evening sky. When at last he settled down in the little field where he usually rested, and thrust his tail into the brook, the steam arose like a cloud, and the water of the stream ran hot through the town. The citizens were greatly frightened, and bitterly blamed the old man for telling about the Minor Canon.

"It is plain," they said, "that the Griffin intended at last to go and look for him, and we should have been saved. Now who can tell what misery you have brought upon us."

The Griffin did not remain long in the little field. As soon as his tail was cool he flew to the town-hall and rang the bell. The citizens knew that they were expected to come there, and although they were afraid to go, they were still more afraid to stay away; and they crowded into the hall. The Griffin was on the platform at one end, flapping his wings and walking up and down, and the end of his tail was still so warm that it slightly scorched the boards as he dragged it after him.

When everybody who was able to come was there, the Griffin stood still and addressed the meeting.

"I have had a contemptible opinion of you," he said, " ever since I discovered what cowards you are, but I had no idea that you were so ungrateful, selfish, and cruel, as I now find you to be. Here was your Minor Canon, who labored day and night for your good, and thought of nothing else but how he might benefit you and make you happy; and as soon as you

imagine yourselves threatened with a danger, — for
well I know you are dreadfully afraid of me, — you
send him off, caring not whether he returns or per-
ishes, hoping thereby to save yourselves. Now, I had
conceived a great liking for that young man, and had
intended, in a day or two, to go and look him up. But
I have changed my mind about him. I shall go and
find him, but I shall send him back here to live among
you, and I intend that he shall enjoy the reward of his
labor and his sacrifices. Go, some of you, to the officers of the church, who so cowardly ran away when I
first came here, and tell them never to return to this
town under penalty of death. And if, when your
Minor Canon comes back to you, you do not bow yourselves before him, put him in the highest place among
you, and serve and honor him all his life, beware of
my terrible vengeance ! There were only two good
things in this town : the Minor Canon and the stone
image of myself over your church-door. One of these
you have sent away, and the other I shall carry away
myself.''

With these words he dismissed the meeting, and it
was time, for the end of his tail had become so hot that
there was danger of its setting fire to the building.

The next morning, the Griffin came to the church,
and tearing the stone image of himself from its fasten-
ings over the great door, he grasped it with his powerful fore-legs and flew up into the air. Then, after
hovering over the town for a moment, he gave his tail
an angry shake and took up his flight to the dreadful
wilds. When he reached this desolate region, he set

the stone Griffin upon a ledge of a rock which rose in front of the dismal cave he called his home. There the image occupied a position somewhat similar to that it had had over the church-door; and the Griffin, panting with the exertion of carrying such an enormous load to so great a distance, lay down upon the ground, and regarded it with much satisfaction. When he felt somewhat rested he went to look for the Minor Canon. He found the young man, weak and half starved, lying under the shadow of a rock. After picking him up and carrying him to his cave, the Griffin flew away to a distant marsh, where he procured some roots and herbs which he well knew were strengthening and beneficial to man, though he had never tasted them himself. After eating these the Minor Canon was greatly revived, and sat up and listened while the Griffin told him what had happened in the town.

" Do you know," said the monster, when he had finished, " that I have had, and still have, a great liking for you?"

" I am very glad to hear it," said the Minor Canon, with his usual politeness.

" I am not at all sure that you would be," said the Griffin, " if you thoroughly understood the state of the case, but we will not consider that now. If some things were different, other things would be otherwise. I have been so enraged by discovering the manner in which you have been treated that I have determined that you shall at last enjoy the rewards and honors to which you are entitled. Lie down and have a good sleep, and then I will take you back to the town."

As he heard these words, a look of trouble came over the young man's face.

"You need not give yourself any anxiety," said the Griffin, "about my return to the town. I shall not remain there. Now that I have that admirable likeness of myself in front of my cave, where I can sit at my leisure, and gaze upon its noble features and magnificent proportions, I have no wish to see that abode of cowardly and selfish people."

The Minor Canon, relieved from his fears, lay back, and dropped into a doze; and when he was sound asleep the Griffin took him up, and carried him back to the town. He arrived just before day-break, and putting the young man gently on the grass in the little field where he himself used to rest, the monster, without having been seen by any of the people, flew back to his home.

When the Minor Canon made his appearance in the morning among the citizens, the enthusiasm and cordiality with which he was received were truly wonderful. He was taken to a house which had been occupied by one of the banished high officers of the place, and every one was anxious to do all that could be done for his health and comfort. The people crowded into the church when he held services, so that the three old women who used to be his week-day congregation could not get to the best seats, which they had always been in the habit of taking; and the parents of the bad children determined to reform them at home, in order that he might be spared the trouble of keeping up his former school. The Minor Canon was appointed to the highest office of the old church, and before he died, he became a bishop.

During the first years after his return from the dreadful wilds, the people of the town looked up to him as a man to whom they were bound to do honor and reverence ; but they often, also, looked up to the sky to see if there were any signs of the Griffin coming back. However, in the course of time, they learned to honor and reverence their former Minor Canon without the fear of being punished if they did not do so.

But they need never have been afraid of the Griffin. The autumnal equinox day came round, and the monster ate nothing. If he could not have the Minor Canon, he did not care for any thing. So, lying down, with his eyes fixed upon the great stone griffin, he gradually declined, and died. It was a good thing for some of the people of the town that they did not know this.

If you should ever visit the old town, you would still see the little griffins on the sides of the church ; but the great stone griffin that was over the door is gone.

OLD PIPES AND THE DRYAD.

A MOUNTAIN brook ran through a little village. Over the brook there was a narrow bridge, and from the bridge a foot-path led out from the village and up the hill-side, to the cottage of Old Pipes and his mother. For many, many years, Old Pipes had been employed by the villagers to pipe the cattle down from the hills. Every afternoon, an hour before sunset, he would sit on a rock in front of his cottage and play on his pipes. Then all the flocks and herds that were grazing on the mountains would hear him, wherever they might happen to be, and would come down to the village — the cows by the easiest paths, the sheep by those not quite so easy, and the goats by the steep and rocky ways that were hardest of all.

But now, for a year or more, Old Pipes had not piped the cattle home. It is true that every afternoon he sat upon the rock and played upon his familiar instrument; but the cattle did not hear him. He had grown old, and his breath was feeble. The echoes of his cheerful notes, which used to come from the rocky hill on the other side of the valley, were heard no more; and twenty yards from Old Pipes one could scarcely tell what tune he was playing. He had become somewhat deaf, and did not know that the sound of his pipes was so thin and weak, and that the cattle did not hear him. The cows, the sheep, and the goats came down every afternoon as before, but this was because two boys and a girl were sent up after them. The villagers did not wish the good old man to know that his piping was no longer of any use, so they paid him his little salary every month, and said nothing about the two boys and the girl.

Old Pipes's mother was, of course, a great deal older then he was, and was as deaf as a gate, — posts, latch, hinges, and all, — and she never knew that the sound of her son's pipe did not spread over all the mountain-side, and echo back strong and clear from the opposite hills. She was very fond of Old Pipes, and proud of his piping; and as he was so much younger than she was, she never thought of him as being very old. She cooked for him, and made his bed, and mended his clothes; and they lived very comfortably on his little salary.

One afternoon, at the end of the month, when Old Pipes had finished his piping, he took his stout staff and went down the hill to the village to receive the money for his month's work. The path seemed a great deal steeper and more difficult than it used to be; and Old Pipes thought that it must have been washed by the rains and greatly damaged. He remembered it as a path that was quite easy to traverse either up or down. But Old Pipes had been a very active man, and as his mother was so much older than he was, he never thought of himself as aged and infirm.

When the Chief Villager had paid him, and he had talked a little with some of his friends, Old Pipes started to go home. But when he had crossed the bridge over the brook, and gone a short distance up the hill-side, he became very tired, and sat down upon a stone. He had not been sitting there half a minute, when along came two boys and a girl.

"Children," said Old Pipes, "I'm very tired to-night, and I don't believe I can climb up this steep path to my home. I think I shall have to ask you to help me."

"We will do that," said the boys and the girl, quite cheerfully; and one boy took him by the right hand, and the other by the left, while the girl pushed him in the back. In this way he went up the hill quite easily, and soon reached his cottage door. Old Pipes gave each of the three children a copper coin, and then they sat down for a few minutes' rest before starting back to the village.

"I'm sorry that I tired you so much," said Old Pipes.

"Oh, that would not have tired us," said one of the boys, "if we had not been so far to-day after the cows, the sheep, and the goats. They rambled high up on the mountain, and we never before had such a time in finding them."

"Had to go after the cows, the sheep, and the goats!" exclaimed Old Pipes. "What do you mean by that?"

The girl, who stood behind the old man, shook her head, put her hand on her mouth, and made all sorts of signs to the boy to stop talking on this subject; but he did not notice her, and promptly answered Old Pipes.

"Why, you see, good sir," said he, "that as the cattle can't hear your pipes now, somebody has to go after them every evening to drive them down from the mountain, and the Chief Villager has hired us three to do it. Generally it is not very hard work, but to-night the cattle had wandered far."

"How long have you been doing this?" asked the old man.

The girl shook her head and clapped her hand on her mouth more vigorously than before, but the boy went on.

"I think it is about a year now," he said, "since the people first felt sure that the cattle could not hear your pipes; and from that time we've been driving them down. But we are rested now, and will go home. Good-night, sir."

The three children then went down the hill, the girl scolding the boy all the way home. Old Pipes stood silent a few moments, and then he went into his cottage.

"Mother," he shouted; "did you hear what those children said?"

"Children!" exclaimed the old woman; "I did not hear them. I did not know there were any children here."

Then Old Pipes told his mother, shouting very loudly to make her hear, how the two boys and the girl had helped him up the hill, and what he had heard about his piping and the cattle.

"They can't hear you?" cried his mother. "Why, what's the matter with the cattle?"

"Ah, me!" said Old Pipes; "I don't believe there's any thing the matter with the cattle. It must be with me and my pipes that there is something the matter. But one thing is certain, if I do not earn the wages the Chief Villager pays me, I shall not take them. I shall go straight down to the village and give back the money I received to-day."

"Nonsense!" cried his mother. "I'm sure you've piped as well as you could, and no more can be expected. And what are we to do without the money?"

"I don't know," said Old Pipes; "but I'm going down to the village to pay it back."

The sun had now set; but the moon was shining very brightly on the hill-side, and Old Pipes could see his way very well. He did not take the same path by which he had gone before, but followed another, which led among the trees upon the hill-side, and, though longer, was not so steep.

When he had gone about half-way, the old man sat down to rest, leaning his back against a great oak-tree. As he did so, he heard a sound like knocking inside the tree, and then a voice distinctly said:

"Let me out! let me out!"

"Old Pipes instantly forgot that he was tired, and sprang to his feet. "This must be a Dryad-tree!" he exclaimed. "If it is, I'll let her out."

Old Pipes had never, to his knowledge, seen a Dryad-tree, but he knew there were such trees on the hill-sides and the mountains, and that Dryads lived in

them. He knew, too, that in the summer-time, on
those days when the moon rose before the sun went
down, a Dryad could come out of her tree if any one
could find the key which locked her in, and turn it.
Old Pipes closely examined the trunk of the tree,
which stood in the full moonlight. "If I see that
key," he said, " I shall surely turn it." Before long
he perceived a piece of bark standing out from the
tree, which appeared to him very much like the handle
of a key. He took hold of it, and found he could
turn it quite around. As he did so, a large part of
the side of the tree was pushed open, and a beautiful
Dryad stepped quickly out.

For a moment she stood motionless, gazing on the
scene before her, — the tranquil valley, the hills, the
forest, and the mountain-side, all lying in the soft
clear light of the moon. "Oh, lovely! lovely!" she
exclaimed. "How long it is since I have seen any
thing like this!" And then, turning to Old Pipes,
she said: "How good of you to let me out! I am so
happy and so thankful, that I must kiss you, you dear
old man!" And she threw her arms around the neck
of Old Pipes, and kissed him on both cheeks. "You
don't know," she then went on to say, "how doleful
it is to be shut up so long in a tree. I don't mind it
in the winter, for then I am glad to be sheltered, but in
summer it is a rueful thing not to be able to see all the
beauties of the world. And it's ever so long since
I've been let out. People so seldom come this way;
and when they do come at the right time they either
don't hear me, or they are frightened, and run away.

But you, you dear old man, you were not frightened, and you looked and looked for the key, and you let me out, and now I shall not have to go back till winter has come, and the air grows cold. Oh, it is glorious! What can I do for you, to show you how grateful I am?"

"I am very glad," said Old Pipes, "that I let you out, since I see that it makes you so happy; but I must admit that I tried to find the key because I had a great desire to see a Dryad. But if you wish to do something for me, you can, if you happen to be going down toward the village."

"To the village!" exclaimed the Dryad. "I will go anywhere for you, my kind old benefactor."

"Well, then," said Old Pipes, "I wish you would take this little bag of money to the Chief Villager and tell him that Old Pipes cannot receive pay for the services which he does not perform. It is now more than a year that I have not been able to make the cattle hear me, when I piped to call them home. I did not know this until to-night; but now that I know it, I cannot keep the money, and so I send it back." And, handing the little bag to the Dryad, he bade her good-night, and turned toward his cottage.

"Good-night," said the Dryad. "And I thank you over, and over, and over again, you good old man!"

Old Pipes walked toward his home, very glad to be saved the fatigue of going all the way down to the village and back again. "To be sure," he said to himself, "this path does not seem at all steep, and I can walk along it very easily ; but it would have tired me dreadfully to come up all the way from the village, especially as I could not have expected those children to help me again.'' When he reached home, his mother was surprised to see him returning so soon.

''What!'' she exclaimed ; ''have you already come back? What did the Chief Villager say? Did he take the money?''

Old Pipes was just about to tell her that he had sent the money to the village by a Dryad, when he suddenly reflected that his mother would be sure to disapprove such a proceeding, and so he merely said he had sent it by a person whom he had met.

'' And how do you know that the person will ever take it to the Chief Villager?'' cried his mother. '' You will lose it, and the villagers will never get it. Oh, Pipes! Pipes! when will you be old enough to have ordinary common sense?''

Old Pipes considered that as he was already seventy years of age he could scarcely expect to grow any wiser, but he made no remark on this subject; and, saying that he doubted not that the money would go safely to its destination, he sat down to his supper. His mother scolded him roundly, but he did not mind it ; and after supper he went out and sat on a rustic chair in front of the cottage to look at the moonlit village, and to wonder whether or not the Chief Villager really received the money. While he was doing these two things, he went fast asleep.

When Old Pipes left the Dryad, she did not go down to the village with the little bag of money. She held it in her hand, and thought about what she had heard. " This is a good and honest old man," she said ; " and it is a shame that he should lose this money. He looked as if he needed it, and I don't believe the people in the village will take it from one who has served them so long. Often, when in my tree, have I heard the sweet notes of his pipes. I am going to take the money back to him." She did not start immediately, because there were so many beautiful things to look at ; but after a while she went up to the cottage, and, finding Old Pipes asleep in his chair, she slipped the little bag into his coat-pocket, and silently sped away.

The next day, Old Pipes told his mother that he would go up the mountain and cut some wood. He had a right to get wood from the mountain, but for a long time he had been content to pick up the dead branches which lay about his cottage. To-day, however, he felt so strong and vigorous that he thought he would go and cut some fuel that would be better than this. He worked all the morning, and when he came back he did not feel at all tired, and he had a very good appetite for his dinner.

Now, Old Pipes knew a good deal about Dryads, but there was one thing which, although he had heard, he had forgotten. This was, that a kiss from a Dryad made a person ten years younger. The people of the village knew this, and they were very careful not to let any child of ten years or younger, go into the woods where the Dryads were supposed to be ; for, if they should chance to be kissed by one of these tree-nymphs, they would be set back so far that they would cease to exist. A story was told in the village that a very bad boy of eleven once ran away into the woods, and had an adventure of this kind; and when his mother found him he was a little baby of one year old. Taking advantage of her opportunity, she brought him up more carefully than she had done before; and he grew to be a very good boy indeed.

Now, Old Pipes had been kissed twice by the Dryad, once on each cheek, and he therefore felt as vigorous and active as when he was a hale man of fifty. His mother noticed how much work he was doing, and told him that he need not try in that way to make up for the loss of his piping wages; for he would only tire himself out, and get sick. But her son answered that he had not felt so well for years, and that he was quite able to work. In the course of the afternoon, Old Pipes, for the first time that day, put his hand in his coat-pocket, and there, to his amazement, he found the little bag of money. "Well, well!" he exclaimed, "I am stupid, indeed! I really thought that I had seen a Dryad; but when I sat down by that big oak-tree I must have gone to sleep and dreamed it all; and then I came home thinking I had given the money to a Dryad, when it was in my pocket all the time. But the Chief Villager shall have the money. I shall not take it to him to-day, but to-morrow I wish to go to the village to see some of my old friends; and then I shall give up the money."

Toward the close of the afternoon, Old Pipes, as had been his custom for so many years, took his pipes from the shelf on which they lay, and went out to the rock in front of the cottage.

"What are you going to do?" cried his mother. "If you will not consent to be paid, why do you pipe?"

"I am going to pipe for my own pleasure," said her son. "I am used to it, and I do not wish to give it up. It does not matter now whether the cattle hear me or not, and I am sure that my piping will injure no one."

When the good man began to play upon his favorite instrument he was astonished at the sound that came from it. The beautiful notes of the pipes sounded clear and strong down into the valley, and spread over the hills, and up the sides of the mountain beyond, while, after a little interval, an echo came back from the rocky hill on the other side of the valley.

"Ha! ha!" he cried, "what has happened to my pipes? They must have been stopped up of late, but now they are as clear and good as ever."

Again the merry notes went sounding far and wide. The cattle on the mountain heard them, and those that were old enough remembered how these notes had called them from their pastures every evening, and so they started down the mountain-side, the others following.

The merry notes were heard in the village below, and the people were much astonished thereby. "Why, who can be blowing the pipes of Old Pipes?" they said. But, as they were all very busy, no one went up to see. One thing, however, was plain enough: the cattle were coming down the mountain. And so the two boys and the girl did not have to go after them, and had an hour for play, for which they were very glad.

The next morning Old Pipes started down to the village with his money, and on the way he met the Dryad. "Oh, ho!" he cried, "is that you? Why, I thought my letting you out of the tree was nothing but a dream."

"A dream!" cried the Dryad; "if you only knew how happy you have made me, you would not think it merely a dream. And has it not benefited you? Do you not feel happier? Yesterday I heard you playing beautifully on your pipes."

"Yes, yes," cried he. "I did not understand it before, but I see it all now. I have really grown younger. I thank you, I thank you, good Dryad, from the bottom of my heart. It was the finding of the money in my pocket that made me think it was a dream."

"Oh, I put it in when you were asleep," she said, laughing, "because I thought you ought to keep it. Good-by, kind, honest man. May you live long, and be as happy as I am now."

Old Pipes was greatly delighted when he understood that he was really a younger man; but that made no difference about the money, and he kept on his way to the village. As soon as he reached it, he was eagerly questioned as to who had been playing his pipes the evening before, and when the people heard that it was himself, they were very much surprised. Thereupon,

Old Pipes told what had happened to him, and then
there was greater wonder, with hearty congratulations
and hand-shakes ; for Old Pipes was liked by every
one. The Chief Villager refused to take his money,
and, although Old Pipes said that he had not earned it,
every one present insisted that, as he would now play
on his pipes as before, he should lose nothing, because,
for a time, he was unable to perform his duty.

So Old Pipes was obliged to keep his money, and
after an hour or two spent in conversation with his
friends, he returned to his cottage.

There was one individual, however, who was not at
all pleased with what had happened to Old Pipes.
This was an Echo-dwarf, who lived on the hills on the
other side of the valley, and whose duty it was to echo
back the notes of the pipes whenever they could be
heard. There were a great many other Echo-dwarfs
on these hills, some of whom echoed back the songs
of maidens, some the shouts of children, and others
the music that was often heard in the village. But
there was only one who could send back the strong
notes of the pipes of Old Pipes, and this had been his
sole duty for many years. But when the old man
grew feeble, and the notes of his pipes could not be
heard on the opposite hills, this Echo-dwarf had nothing to do, and he spent his time in delightful idleness ;
and he slept so much and grew so fat that it made his
companions laugh to see him walk.

On the afternoon on which, after so long an interval,
the sound of the pipes was heard on the echo hills,
this dwarf was fast asleep behind a rock. As soon as

the first notes reached them, some of his companions
ran to wake him. Rolling to his feet, he echoed back
the merry tune of Old Pipes. Naturally, he was very
much annoyed and indignant at being thus obliged to
give up his life of comfortable leisure, and he hoped
very much that this pipe-playing would not occur again.
The next afternoon he was awake and listening, and,
sure enough, at the usual hour, along came the notes
of the pipes as clear and strong as they ever had been ;
and he was obliged to work as long as Old Pipes
played. The Echo-dwarf was very angry. He had
supposed, of course, that the pipe-playing had ceased
forever, and he felt that he had a right to be indignant
at being thus deceived. He was so much disturbed
that he made up his mind to go and try to find out
whether this was to be a temporary matter or not.
He had plenty of time, as the pipes were played but
once a day, and he set off early in the morning for
the hill on which Old Pipes lived. It was hard work
for the fat little fellow, and when he had crossed the
valley and had gone some distance into the woods on
the hill-side, he stopped to rest, and, in a few minutes,
the Dryad came tripping along.

"Ho, ho!" exclaimed the dwarf; "what are you
doing here? and how did you get out of your
tree?"

"Doing!" cried the Dryad; "I am being happy;
that's what I am doing. And I was let out of my
tree by the good old man who plays the pipes to call
the cattle down from the mountain. And it makes me
happier to think that I have been of service to him.

I gave him two kisses of gratitude, and now he is young enough to play his pipes as well as ever.''

The Echo-dwarf stepped forward, his face pale with passion. '' Am I to believe,'' he said, '' that you are the cause of this great evil that has come upon me? and that you are the wicked creature who has again started this old man upon his career of pipe-playing? What have I ever done to you that you should have condemned me for years and years to echo back the notes of those wretched pipes? ''

At this the Dryad laughed loudly.

'' What a funny little fellow you are! '' she said. '' Any one would think you had been condemned to toil from morning till night; while what you really have to do is merely to imitate for half an hour every day the merry notes of Old Pipes's piping. Fie upon you, Echo-dwarf! You are lazy and selfish; and that is what is the matter with you. Instead of grumbling at being obliged to do a little wholesome work, which is less, I am sure, than that of any other echo-dwarf upon the rocky hill-side, you should rejoice at the good fortune of the old man who has regained so much of his strength and vigor. Go home and learn to be just and generous; and then, perhaps, you may be happy. Good-by.''

'' Insolent creature! '' shouted the dwarf, as he shook his fat little fist at her. '' I'll make you suffer for this. You shall find out what it is to heap injury and insult upon one like me, and to snatch from him the repose that he has earned by long years of toil.''

And, shaking his head savagely, he hurried back to the rocky hill-side.

Every afternoon the merry notes of the pipes of Old Pipes sounded down into the valley and over the hills and up the mountain-side; and every afternoon when he had echoed them back, the little dwarf grew more and more angry with the Dryad. Each day, from early morning till it was time for him to go back to his duties upon the rocky hill-side, he searched the woods for her. He intended, if he met her, to pretend to be very sorry for what he had said, and he thought he might be able to play a trick upon her which would avenge him well. One day, while thus wandering among the trees, he met Old Pipes. The Echo-dwarf did not generally care to see or speak to ordinary people; but now he was so anxious to find the object of his search, that he stopped and asked Old Pipes if he had seen the Dryad. The piper had not noticed the little fellow, and he looked down on him with some surprise.

"No," he said; "I have not seen her, and I have been looking everywhere for her."

"You!" cried the dwarf, "what do you wish with her?"

Old Pipes then sat down on a stone, so that he should be nearer the ear of his small companion, and he told what the Dryad had done for him.

When the Echo-dwarf heard that this was the man whose pipes he was obliged to echo back every day, he would have slain him on the spot had he been able; but, as he was not able, he merely ground his teeth and listened to the rest of the story.

" I am looking for the Dryad now," Old Pipes continued, " on account of my aged mother. When I was old myself, I did not notice how very old my mother was; but now it shocks me to see how feeble and decrepit her years have caused her to become; and I am looking for the Dryad to ask her to make my mother younger, as she made me."

The eyes of the Echo-dwarf glistened. Here was a man who might help him in his plans.

" Your idea is a good one," he said to Old Pipes, " and it does you honor. But you should know that a Dryad can make no person younger but one who lets her out of her tree. However, you can manage the affair very easily. All you need do is to find the Dryad, tell her what you want, and request her to step into her tree and be shut up for a short time. Then you will go and bring your mother to the tree; she will open it, and every thing will be as you wish. Is not this a good plan? "

" Excellent! " cried Old Pipes; " and I will go instantly and search more diligently for the Dryad."

" Take me with you," said the Echo-dwarf. " You can easily carry me on your strong shoulders; and I shall be glad to help you in any way that I can."

" Now, then," said the little fellow to himself, as Old Pipes carried him rapidly along, " if he persuades the Dryad to get into a tree, — and she is quite foolish enough to do it, — and then goes away to bring his mother, I shall take a stone or a club and I will break off the key of that tree, so that nobody can ever turn it again. Then Mistress Dryad will see what she has brought upon herself by her behavior to me."

Before long they came to the great oak-tree in which the Dryad had lived, and, at a distance, they saw that beautiful creature herself coming toward them.

"How excellently well every thing happens!" said the dwarf. "Put me down, and I will go. Your business with the Dryad is more important than mine; and you need not say any thing about my having suggested your plan to you. I am willing that you should have all the credit of it yourself."

Old Pipes put the Echo-dwarf upon the ground, but the little rogue did not go away. He concealed himself between some low, mossy rocks, and he was so much of their color that you would not have noticed him if you had been looking straight at him.

When the Dryad came up, Old Pipes lost no time in telling her about his mother, and what he wished her to do. At first, the Dryad answered nothing, but stood looking very sadly at Old Pipes.

"Do you really wish me to go into my tree again?" she said. "I should dreadfully dislike to do it, for I don't know what might happen. It is not at all necessary, for I could make your mother younger at any time if she would give me the opportunity. I had already thought of making you still happier in this way, and several times I have waited about your cottage, hoping to meet your aged mother, but she never comes outside, and you know a Dryad cannot enter a house. I cannot imagine what put this idea into your head. Did you think of it yourself?"

"No, I cannot say that I did," answered Old

Pipes. "A little dwarf whom I met in the woods proposed it to me."

"Oh!" cried the Dryad; "now I see through it all. It is the scheme of that vile Echo-dwarf — your enemy and mine. Where is he? I should like to see him."

"I think he has gone away," said Old Pipes.

"No he has not," said the Dryad, whose quick eyes perceived the Echo-dwarf among the rocks. "There he is. Seize him and drag him out, I beg of you."

Old Pipes perceived the dwarf as soon as he was pointed out to him, and, running to the rocks, he caught the little fellow by the arm and pulled him out.

"Now, then," cried the Dryad, who had opened the door of the great oak, "just stick him in there, and we will shut him up. Then I shall be safe from his mischief for the rest of the time I am free."

Old Pipes thrust the Echo-dwarf into the tree; the Dryad pushed the door shut; there was a clicking sound of bark and wood, and no one would have noticed that the big oak had ever had an opening in it.

"There," said the Dryad; "now we need not be afraid of him. And I assure you, my good piper, that I shall be very glad to make your mother younger as soon as I can. Will you not ask her to come out and meet me?"

"Of course I will," cried Old Pipes; "and I will do it without delay."

And then, the Dryad by his side, he hurried to his

cottage. But when he mentioned the matter to his mother, the old woman became very angry indeed. She did not believe in Dryads; and, if they really did exist, she knew they must be witches and sorceresses, and she would have nothing to do with them. If her son had ever allowed himself to be kissed by one of them, he ought to be ashamed of himself. As to its doing him the least bit of good, she did not believe a word of it. He felt better than he used to feel, but that was very common. She had sometimes felt that way herself, and she forbade him ever to mention a Dryad to her again.

That afternoon, Old Pipes, feeling very sad that his plan in regard to his mother had failed, sat down upon the rock and played upon his pipes. The pleasant sounds went down the valley and up the hills and mountain, but, to the great surprise of some persons who happened to notice the fact, the notes were not echoed back from the rocky hill-side, but from the woods on the side of the valley on which Old Pipes lived. The next day many of the villagers stopped in their work to listen to the echo of the pipes coming from the woods. The sound was not as clear and strong as it used to be when it was sent back from the rocky hill-side, but it certainly came from among the trees. Such a thing as an echo changing its place in this way had never been heard of before, and nobody was able to explain how it could have happened. Old Pipes, however, knew very well that the sound came from the Echo-dwarf shut up in the great oak-tree. The sides of the tree were thin, and the sound of the

pipes could be heard through them, and the dwarf was
obliged by the laws of his being to echo back those
notes whenever they came to him. But Old Pipes
thought he might get the Dryad in trouble if he let any
one know that the Echo-dwarf was shut up in the tree,
and so he wisely said nothing about it.

One day the two boys and the girl who had helped
Old Pipes up the hill were playing in the woods. Stop-
ping near the great oak-tree, they heard a sound of
knocking within it, and then a voice plainly said:

" Let me out! let me out!"

For a moment the children stood still in astonishment, and then one of the boys exclaimed:

" Oh, it is a Dryad, like the one Old Pipes found!
Let's let her out!"

" What are you thinking of?" cried the girl. " I
am the oldest of all, and I am only thirteen. Do you
wish to be turned into crawling babies? Run! run!
run!"

And the two boys and the girl dashed down into the
valley as fast as their legs could carry them. There
was no desire in their youthful hearts to be made
younger than they were. And for fear that their parents might think it well that they should commence
their careers anew, they never said a word about
finding the Dryad-tree.

As the summer days went on, Old Pipes's mother
grew feebler and feebler. One day when her son was
away, for he now frequently went into the woods to
hunt or fish, or down into the valley to work, she arose
from her knitting to prepare the simple dinner. But

she felt so weak and tired that she was not able to
do the work to which she had been so long accustomed.
" Alas! alas!" she said, " the time has come when I
am too old to work. My son will have to hire some
one to come here and cook his meals, make his bed,
and mend his clothes. Alas! alas! I had hoped that
as long as I lived I should be able to do these things.
But it is not so. I have grown utterly worthless, and
some one else must prepare the dinner for my son. I
wonder where he is." And tottering to the door, she
went outside to look for him. She did not feel able to
stand, and reaching the rustic chair, she sank into it,
quite exhausted, and soon fell asleep.

The Dryad, who had often come to the cottage to
see if she could find an opportunity of carrying out old
Pipes's affectionate design, now happened by; and
seeing that the much-desired occasion had come, she
stepped up quietly behind the old woman and gently
kissed her on each cheek, and then as quietly dis
appeared.

In a few minutes the mother of old Pipes awoke, and
looking up at the sun, she exclaimed : " Why, it is
almost dinner-time! My son will be here directly, and
I am not ready for him." And rising to her feet, she
hurried into the house, made the fire, set the meat and
vegetables to cook, laid the cloth, and by the time her
son arrived the meal was on the table.

" How a little sleep does refresh one," she said to
herself, as she was bustling about. She was a woman
of very vigorous constitution, and at seventy had been
a great deal stronger and more active than her son was

at that age. The moment Old Pipes saw his mother, he knew that the Dryad had been there; but, while he felt as happy as a king, he was too wise to say any thing about her.

"It is astonishing how well I feel to-day," said his mother; "and either my hearing has improved or you speak much more plainly than you have done of late."

The summer days went on and passed away, the leaves were falling from the trees, and the air was becoming cold.

"Nature has ceased to be lovely," said the Dryad, "and the night-winds chill me. It is time for me to go back into my comfortable quarters in the great oak. But first I must pay another visit to the cottage of old Pipes."

She found the piper and his mother sitting side by side on the rock in front of the door. The cattle were not to go to the mountain any more that season, and he was piping them down for the last time. Loud and merrily sounded the pipes of Old Pipes, and down the mountain-side came the cattle, the cows by the easiest paths, the sheep by those not quite so easy, and the goats by the most difficult ones among the rocks; while from the great oak-tree were heard the echoes of the cheerful music.

"How happy they look, sitting there together," said the Dryad; "and I don't believe it will do them a bit of harm to be still younger." And moving quietly up behind them, she first kissed Old Pipes on his cheek and then his mother.

Old Pipes, who had stopped playing, knew what it

was, but he did not move, and said nothing. His
mother, thinking that her son had kissed her, turned
to him with a smile and kissed him in return. And
then she arose and went into the cottage, a vigorous
woman of sixty, followed by her son, erect and happy,
and twenty years younger than herself.

The Dryad sped away to the woods, shrugging her
shoulders as she felt the cool evening wind.

When she reached the great oak, she turned the key
and opened the door. "Come out," she said to the
Echo-dwarf, who sat blinking within. "Winter is
coming on, and I want the comfortable shelter of my
tree for myself. The cattle have come down from the
mountain for the last time this year, the pipes will no
longer sound, and you can go to your rocks and have
a holiday until next spring."

Upon hearing these words the dwarf skipped quickly
out, and the Dryad entered the tree and pulled the
door shut after her. "Now, then," she said to herself, "he can break off the key if he likes. It does
not matter to me. Another will grow out next spring.
And although the good piper made me no promise, I
know that when the warm days arrive next year, he
will come and let me out again."

The Echo-dwarf did not stop to break the key of the
tree. He was too happy to be released to think of any
thing else, and he hastened as fast as he could to his
home on the rocky hill-side.

The Dryad was not mistaken when she trusted in
the piper. When the warm days came again he went

to the oak-tree to let her out.   But, to his sorrow and surprise, he found the great tree lying upon the ground.   A winter storm had blown it down, and it lay with its trunk shattered and split.   And what became of the Dryad, no one ever knew.

THE QUEEN'S MUSEUM.

THERE was once a Queen who founded, in her capital city, a grand museum. This institution was the pride of her heart, and she devoted nearly all her time to overseeing the collection of objects for it, and their arrangement in the spacious halls. This museum was intended to elevate the intelligence of her people, but the result was quite disappointing to the Queen. For some reason, and what it was she could not imagine, the people were not interested in her museum. She considered it the most delightful place in the world, and spent hours every day in examining and studying the thousands of objects it contained; but although here and there in the city there was a person who cared to visit the collection, the great body of the people found it impossible to feel the slightest interest in it. At first this grieved the Queen, and she tried to make her museum better; but as this did no good, she became very angry, and she issued a decree that all persons of mature age who were not interested in her museum should be sent to prison.

This decree produced a great sensation in the city. The people crowded to the building, and did their very best to be interested; but, in the majority of cases, the attempt was an utter failure. They could not feel any interest whatever. The consequence was that hundreds and thousands of the people were sent to prison, and as there was not room enough for them in the ordinary jails, large temporary prisons were erected in various parts of the city. Those persons who were actually needed for work or service which no one else could do were allowed to come out in the day-time on parole; but at night they had to return to their prisons.

It was during this deplorable state of affairs that a stranger entered the city one day. He was surprised at seeing so many prisons, and approaching the window in one of them, behind the bars of which he saw a very respectable-looking citizen, he asked what all this meant. The citizen informed him how matters stood, and then, with tears mounting to his eyes, he added:

" Oh, sir, I have tried my best to be interested in that museum; but it is impossible; I cannot make myself care for it in the slightest degree! And, what is more, I know I shall never be able to do so; and I shall languish here for the rest of my days."

Passing on, the Stranger met a mother coming out of her house. Her face was pale, and she was weeping bitterly. Filled with pity, he stopped and asked her what was the matter. " Oh, sir," she said, " for a week I have been trying, for the sake of my dear children, to take an interest in that museum. For a time I thought I might do it, but the hopes proved false. It is impossible. I must leave my little ones, and go to prison."

The Stranger was deeply affected by these cases and many others of a similar character, which he soon met with. "It is too bad! too bad!" he said to himself. "I never saw a city in so much trouble. There is scarcely a family, I am told, in which there is not some uninterested person — I must see the Queen and talk to her about it," and with this he wended his way to the palace.

He met the Queen just starting out on her morning visit to the museum. When he made it known that he was a stranger, and desired a short audience, she stopped and spoke to him.

"Have you visited my museum yet?" she said. "There is nothing in the city so well worth your attention as that. You should go there before seeing any thing else. You have a high forehead, and an intelligent expression, and I have no doubt that it will interest you greatly. I am going there myself, and I shall be glad to see what effect that fine collection has upon a stranger."

This did not suit the Stranger at all. From what he had heard he felt quite sure that if he went to the museum, he would soon be in jail; and so he hurried to propose a plan which had occurred to him while on his way to the palace.

"I came to see your Majesty on the subject of the museum," he said, "and to crave permission to contribute to the collection some objects which shall be interesting to every one. I understand that it is highly desirable that every one should be interested."

" Of course it is," said the Queen, " and although I think that there is not the slightest reason why every one should not feel the keenest interest in what the museum already contains, I am willing to add to it whatever may make it of greater value."

" In that case," said the Stranger, " no time should be lost in securing what I wish to present."

" Go at once," said the Queen. " But how soon can you return? "

" It will take some days, at least," said the Stranger.

" Give me your parole to return in a week," said the Queen, " and start immediately."

The Stranger gave his parole and left the palace. Having filled a leathern bag with provisions from a cook's shop, he went out of the city gates. As he walked into the open country, he said to himself :

" I have certainly undertaken a very difficult enterprise. Where I am to find any thing that will interest all the people in that city, I am sure I do not know ; but my heart is so filled with pity for the great number of unfortunate persons who are torn from their homes and shut up in prison, that I am determined to do something for them, if I possibly can. There must be some objects to be found in this vast country that will interest every one."

About noon he came to a great mountain-side covered with a forest. Thinking that he was as likely to find what he sought in one place as another, and preferring the shade to the sun, he entered the forest, and walked for some distance along a path which gradually led up the mountain. Having crossed a brook with its edges lined with water-cresses, he soon perceived a large cave, at the entrance of which sat an aged hermit. "Ah," said the Stranger to himself, "this is indeed fortunate! This good and venerable man, who passes his life amid the secrets of nature, can surely tell me what I wish to know." Saluting the Hermit, he sat down and told the old man the object of his quest.

"I am afraid you are looking for what you will not find," said the Hermit. "Most people are too silly to be truly interested in any thing. They herd together like cattle, and do not know what is good for them. There are now on this mountain-side many commodious and comfortable caves, all of which would be tenanted if people only knew how improving and interesting it is to live apart from their fellow-men. But, so far as it can be done, I will help you in your quest, which I think is a worthy one. I can do nothing for you myself, but I have a pupil who is very much given to wandering about, and looking for curious things. He may tell you where you will be able to find something that will interest everybody, though I doubt it. You may go and see him, if you like, and I will excuse him from his studies for a time, so that he may aid you in your search."

The Hermit then wrote an excuse upon a piece of parchment, and, giving it to the Stranger, he directed him to the cave of his pupil.

This was situated at some distance, and higher up the mountain, and when the Stranger reached it, he found the Pupil fast asleep upon the ground. This individual was a long-legged youth, with long arms, long hair, a long nose, and a long face. When the Stranger awakened him, told him why he had come, and gave him the hermit's excuse, the sleepy eyes of the Pupil brightened, and his face grew less long.

" That's delightful ! " he said, " to be let off on a Monday; for I generally have to be satisfied with a half-holiday, Wednesdays and Saturdays."

" Is the Hermit very strict with you?" asked the Stranger.

" Yes," said the Pupil, " I have to stick closely to the cave ; though I have been known to go fishing on days when there was no holiday. I have never seen the old man but once, and that was when he first took me. You know it wouldn't do for us to be too sociable. That would n't be hermit-like. He comes up here on the afternoons I am out, and writes down what I am to do for the next half-week."

" And do you always do it?" asked the Stranger.

" Oh, I get some of it done," said the Pupil; " but there have been times when I have wondered whether it wouldn't have been better for me to have been something else. But I have chosen my profession, and I suppose I must be faithful to it. We will start immediately on our search; but first I must put the cave in order, for the old man will be sure to come up while I am gone."

So saying, the Pupil opened an old parchment book

at a marked page, and laid it on a flat stone, which served as a table, and then placed a skull and a couple of bones in a proper position near by.

The two now started off, the Pupil first putting a line and hook in his pocket, and pulling out a fishing-rod from under some bushes.

"What do you want with that?" asked the Stranger, "we are not going to fish!"

"Why not?" said the Pupil; "if we come to a good place, we might catch something that would be a real curiosity."

Before long they came to a mountain brook, and here the Pupil insisted on trying his luck. The Stranger was a little tired and hungry, and so was quite willing to sit down for a time and eat something from his bag. The Pupil ran off to find some bait, and he staid away so long that the Stranger had quite finished his meal before he returned. He came back at last, however, in a state of great excitement.

"Come with me! come with me!" he cried. "I have found something that is truly astonishing! Come quickly!"

The Stranger arose and hurried after the Pupil, whose long legs carried him rapidly over the mountain-side. Reaching a large hole at the bottom of a precipitous rock, the Pupil stopped, and exclaiming: "Come in here and I will show you something that will amaze you!" he immediately entered the hole.

The Stranger, who was very anxious to see what curiosity he had found, followed him some distance along a narrow and winding under-ground passage.

The two suddenly emerged into a high and spacious cavern, which was lighted by openings in the roof; on the floor, in various places, were strongly fastened boxes, and packages of many sorts, bales and bundles of silks and rich cloths, with handsome caskets, and many other articles of value.

"What kind of a place is this?" exclaimed the Stranger, in great surprise.

"Don't you know?" cried the Pupil, his eyes fairly sparkling with delight. "It is a robber's den! Isn't it a great thing to find a place like this?"

"A robber's den!" exclaimed the Stranger in alarm; "let us get out of it as quickly as we can, or the robbers will return, and we shall be cut to pieces."

"I don't believe they are coming back very soon," said the Pupil, "and we ought to stop and take a look at some of these things."

"Fly, you foolish youth!" cried the Stranger; "you do not know what danger you are in." And, so saying, he turned to hasten away from the place.

But he was too late. At that moment the robber captain and his band entered the cave. When these men perceived the Stranger and the Hermit's Pupil, they drew their swords and were about to rush upon them, when the Pupil sprang forward and, throwing up his long arms, exclaimed:

' Stop ! it is a mistake ! "

At these words, the robber captain lowered his sword, and motioned to his men to halt. "A mistake!" he said; "what do you mean by that?"

"I mean," said the Pupil, "that I was out looking

for curiosities, and wandered into this place by acci-
dent. We haven't taken a thing. You may count your
goods, and you will find nothing missing. We have
not even opened a box, although I very much wanted
to see what was in some of them."

"Are his statements correct?" said the Captain,
turning to the Stranger.

"Entirely so," was the answer.

"You have truthful features, and an honest expression," said the Captain, "and I do not believe you
would be so dishonorable as to creep in here during
our absence and steal our possessions. Your lives
shall be spared, but you will be obliged to remain
with us; for we cannot allow any one who knows our
secret to leave us. You shall be treated well, and
shall accompany us in our expeditions; and if your
conduct merits it, you shall in time be made full
members."

Bitterly the Stranger now regretted his unfortunate
position. He strode up and down one side of the cave,
vowing inwardly that never again would he allow himself to be led by a Hermit's Pupil. That individual,
however, was in a state of high delight. He ran
about from box to bale, looking at the rare treasures
which some of the robbers showed him.

The two captives were fed and lodged very well;
and the next day the Captain called them and the
band together, and addressed them.

"We are now twenty-nine in number," he said;
"twenty-seven full members, and two on probation.
To-night we are about to undertake a very important

expedition, in which we shall all join. We shall fasten up the door of the cave, and at the proper time I shall tell you to what place we are going."

An hour or two before midnight the band set out, accompanied by the Stranger and the Hermit's Pupil; and when they had gone some miles the Captain halted them to inform them of the object of the expedition. "We are going," he said, "to rob the Queen's museum. It is the most important business we have ever undertaken."

At these words the Stranger stepped forward and made a protest. "I left the city yesterday," he said, "commissioned by the Queen to obtain one or more objects of interest for her museum; and to return now to rob an institution which I have promised to enrich will be simply impossible."

"You are right," said the Captain, after a moment's reflection, "such an action would be highly dishonorable on your part. If you will give me your word of honor that you will remain by this stone until our return, the expedition will proceed without you."

The Stranger gave his word, and having been left sitting upon the stone, soon dropped asleep, and so remained until he was awakened by the return of the band, a little before daylight. They came slowly toiling along, each man carrying an enormous bundle upon his back. Near the end of the line was the Hermit's Pupil, bearing a load as heavy as any of the others. The Stranger offered to relieve him for a time of his burden, but the Pupil would not allow it.

"I don't wish these men to think I can't do as much

as they can," he said. "You ought to have been along. We had a fine time! We swept that museum clean, I tell you! We didn't leave a thing on a shelf or in a case."

"What sort of things are they," asked the Stranger.

"I don't know," replied the Pupil, "we didn't have any light for fear people would notice it, but the moon shone in bright enough for us to see all the shelves and the cases; and our orders were not to try and examine any thing, but to take all that was there. The cases had great cloth covers on them, and we spread these on the floor and made bundles of the curiosities. We are going to examine them carefully as soon as we get to the den."

It was broad daylight when the robbers reached their cave. The bundles were laid in a great circle on the floor, and, at a given signal, they were opened. For a moment each robber gazed blankly at the contents of his bundle, and then they all began to fumble and search among the piles of articles upon the cloths; but after a few minutes, they arose, looking blanker and more disappointed than before.

"So far as I can see," said the Captain, "there is nothing in the whole collection that I care for. I do not like a thing here!"

"Nor I!" "Nor I!" "Nor I!" cried each one of his band.

"I suppose," said the Captain, after musing for a moment, "that as these things are of no use to us, we are bound in honor to take them back."

"Hold!" said the Stranger, stepping forward; "do not be in too great a hurry to do that." He then told the Captain of the state of affairs in the city, and explained in full the nature of the expedition he had undertaken for the Queen. "I think it would be better," he said, "if these things were not taken back for the present. If you have a safe place where you can put them, I will in due time tell the Queen where they are, and if she chooses she can send for them."

"Good!" said the Captain, "it is but right that she should bear part of the labor of transportation. There is a disused cave, a mile or so away, and we will tie up these bundles and carry them there; and then we shall leave the matter to you. We take no further interest in it. And if you have given your parole to the Queen to return in a week," the Captain further continued, "of course you'll have to keep it. Did you give your parole also?" he asked, turning to the Pupil.

"Oh, no!" cried that youth; "there was no time fixed for my return. And I am sure that I like a robber's life much better than that of a hermit. There is ever so much more spice and dash in it."

"The Stranger was then told that if he would promise not to betray the robbers he might depart. He gave the promise; but added sadly that he had lost so much time that he was afraid he would not now be able to attain the object of his search and return within the week.

"If that is the case," said the Captain, "we will gladly assist you. "Comrades!" he cried, addressing his band, "after stowing this useless booty in the disused cave, and taking some rest and refreshment, we will set out again, and the object of our expedition shall be to obtain something for the Queen's museum which will interest every one."

Shortly after midnight the robbers set out, accompanied by the Stranger and the Pupil. When they had walked about an hour, the Captain, as was his custom, brought them to a halt that he might tell them where they were going. "I have concluded," said he, "that no place is so likely to contain what we are looking for as the castle of the great magician, Alframedj. We will, therefore, proceed thither, and sack the castle."

"Will there not be great danger in attacking the castle of a magician?" asked the Stranger in somewhat anxious tones.

"Of course there will be," said the Captain, "but we are not such cowards as to hesitate on account of danger. Forward, my men!" And on they all marched.

When they reached the magician's castle, the order was given to scale the outer wall. This the robbers did with great agility, and the Hermit's Pupil was among the first to surmount it. But the Stranger was not used to climbing, and he had to be assisted over the wall. Inside the great court-yard they perceived numbers of Weirds — strange shadowy creatures who gathered silently around them; but not in the least appalled, the robbers formed into a body, and marched into the castle, the door of which stood open. They now entered a great hall, having at one end a doorway before which hung a curtain. Following their Captain, the robbers approached this curtain, and pushing it aside, entered the room beyond. There, behind a large table, sat the great magician, Alfrarmedj, busy over his mystic studies, which he generally pursued in the dead hours of the night. Drawing their swords, the robbers rushed upon him.

" Surrender ! " cried the Captain, " and deliver to us the treasures of your castle."

The old magician raised his head from his book, and, pushing up his spectacles from his forehead, looked at them mildly, and said :

" Freeze ! "

Instantly, they all froze as hard as ice, each man remaining in the position in which he was when the magical word was uttered. With uplifted swords and glaring eyes they stood, rigid and stiff, before the magician. After calmly surveying the group, the old man said :

" I see among you one who has an intelligent brow and truthful expression. His head may thaw sufficiently for him to tell me what means this untimely intrusion upon my studies."

The Stranger now felt his head begin to thaw, and in a few moments he was able to speak. He then told the magician about the Queen's museum, and how it had happened that he had come there with the robbers.

" Your motive is a good one," said the magician, " though your actions are somewhat erratic ; and I do not mind helping you to find what you wish. In what class of objects do the people of the city take the most interest?"

"Truly I do not know," said the Stranger.

"This is indeed surprising!" exclaimed Alfrarmedj. "How can you expect to obtain that which will interest every one, when you do not know what it is in which every one takes an interest? Go, find out this, and then return to me, and I will see what can be done."

The magician then summoned his Weirds and ordered them to carry the frozen visitors outside the castle walls. Each one of the rigid figures was taken up by two Weirds, who carried him out and stood him up in the road outside the castle. When all had been properly set up, with the captain at their head, the gates were shut, and the magician still sitting at his table, uttered the word, "Thaw!"

Instantly, the whole band thawed and marched away. At daybreak they halted, and considered how they should find out what all the people in the city took an interest in.

"One thing is certain," cried the Hermit's Pupil, "whatever it is, it isn't the same thing."

"Your remark is not well put together," said the Stranger, "but I see the force of it. It is true that different people like different things. But how shall we find out what the different people like?"

"By asking them," said the Pupil.

"Good!" cried the Captain, who preferred action to words. "This night we will ask them."

He then drew upon the sand a plan of the city, —
(with which he was quite familiar, having carefully
robbed it for many years,) — and divided it into
twenty-eight sections, each one of which was assigned
to a man. "I omit you," the Captain said to the
Stranger, "because I find that you are not expert
at climbing." He then announced that at night the
band would visit the city, and that each man should
enter the houses in his district, and ask the people
what it was in which they took the greatest interest.

They then proceeded to the cave for rest and
refreshment; and a little before midnight they entered
the city, and each member of the band, including the
Hermit's Pupil, proceeded to attend to the business
assigned to him. It was ordered that no one should
disturb the Queen, for they knew that what she took
most interest in was the museum. During the night
nearly every person in the town was aroused by a
black-bearded robber, who had climbed into one of the
windows of the house, and who, instead of demanding
money and jewels, simply asked what it was in which
that person took the greatest interest. Upon receiv-
ing an answer, the robber repeated it until he had
learned it by heart, and then went to the next house.
As so many of the citizens were confined in prisons,
which the robbers easily entered, they transacted the
business in much less time than they would otherwise
have required.

The Hermit's Pupil was very active, climbing into
and out of houses with great agility. He obtained his
answers quite as easily as did the others, but whenever

he left a house there was a shade of disappointment upon his features. Among the last places that he visited was a room in which two boys were sleeping. He awoke them and asked the usual question. While they were trembling in their bed, not knowing what to answer, the Pupil drew his sword and exclaimed: "Come, now, no prevarication; you know it's fishing-tackle. Speak out!" Each of the boys then promptly declared it was fishing-tackle, and the pupil left, greatly gratified. "I was very much afraid," he said to himself, "that not a person in my district would say fishing-tackle; and I am glad to think that there were two boys who had sense enough to like something that is really interesting."

It was nearly daylight when the work was finished; and then the band gathered together in an appointed place on the outside of the city, where the Stranger awaited them. Each of the men had an excellent memory, which was necessary in their profession, and they repeated to the Stranger all the objects and subjects that had been mentioned to them, and he wrote them down upon tablets.

The next night, accompanied by the band, he proceeded to the castle of the magician, the great gate of which was silently opened for them by the Weirds. When they were ushered into the magician's room, Alfrarmedj took the tablets from the Stranger and examined them carefully.

"All these things should make a very complete collection," he said, "and I think I have specimens of the various objects in my interminable vaults."

He then called his Weirds and, giving one of them the tablets, told him to go with his companions into the vaults and gather enough of the things therein mentioned to fill a large museum. In half an hour the Weirds returned and announced that the articles were ready in the great court-yard.

"Go, then, said the magician, "and assist these men to carry them to the Queen's museum."

The Stranger then heartily thanked Alfrarmedj for the assistance he had given; and the band, accompanied by a number of Weirds, proceeded to carry the objects of interest to the Queen's museum. It was a strange procession. Half a dozen Weirds carried a stuffed mammoth, followed by others bearing the skeleton of a whale, while the robbers and the rest of their queer helpers were loaded with every thing relating to history, science, and art which ought to be in a really good museum. When the whole collection had been put in place upon the floors, the shelves, and in the cases, it was nearly morning. The robbers, with the Hermit's Pupil, retired to the cave; the Weirds disappeared; while the Stranger betook himself to the Queen's palace, where, as soon as the proper hour arrived, he requested an audience.

When he saw the Queen, he perceived that she was very pale and that her cheeks bore traces of recent tears. "You are back in good time," she said to him, "but it makes very little difference whether you have succeeded in your mission or not. There is no longer any museum. There has been a great robbery, and the thieves have carried off the whole of the vast and valuable collection which I have been so long in making."

"I know of that affair," said the Stranger, "and I have already placed in your museum-building the collection which I have obtained. If your Majesty pleases, I shall be glad to have you look at it. It may, in some degree, compensate for that which has been stolen."

"Compensate!" cried the Queen. "Nothing can compensate for it; I do not even wish to see what you have brought."

"Be that as your Majesty pleases," said the Stranger; "but I will be so bold as to say that I have great hopes that the collection which I have obtained will interest the people. Will your Majesty graciously allow them to see it?"

"I have no objection to that," said the Queen; "and indeed I shall be very glad if they can be made to be interested in the museum. I will give orders that the prisons be opened, so that everybody can go to see what you have brought; and those who shall be interested in it may return to their homes. I did not release my obstinate subjects when the museum was robbed, because their fault then was just as great as it was before; and it would not be right that they should profit by my loss."

The Queen's proclamation was made, and for several days the museum was crowded with people moving from morning till night through the vast collection of stuffed animals, birds, and fishes; rare and brilliant insects; mineral and vegetable curiosities; beautiful

works of art; and all the strange, valuable, and in-
structive objects which had been brought from the
interminable vaults of the magician Alfrarmedj. The
Queen's officers, who had been sent to observe whether
or not the people were interested, were in no doubt
upon this point. Every eye sparkled with delight,
for every one found something which was the very
thing he wished to see; and in the throng was the
Hermit's Pupil, standing in rapt ecstasy before a large
case containing all sorts of fishing-tackle, from the
smallest hooks for little minnows to the great irons
and spears used in capturing whales.

No one went back to prison, and the city was full
of re-united households and happy homes. On the
morning of the fourth day, a grand procession of
citizens came to the palace to express to the Queen
their delight and appreciation of her museum. The
great happiness of her subjects could but please the
Queen. She called the Stranger to her, and said to
him:

"Tell me how you came to know what it was that
would interest my people."

"I asked them," said the Stranger. "That is to
say, I arranged that they should be asked."

"That was well done," said the Queen; "but it is
a great pity that my long labors in their behalf should
have been lost. For many years I have been a col-
lector of button-holes; and there was nothing valuable
·or rare in the line of my studies of which I had not
an original specimen or a fac-simile. My agents
brought me from foreign lands, even from the most

distant islands of the sea, button-holes of every kind; in silk, in wool, in cloth of gold, in every imaginable material, and of those which could not be obtained careful copies were made. There was not a duplicate specimen in the whole collection; only one of each kind; nothing repeated. Never before was there such a museum. With all my power I strove to educate my people up to an appreciation of button-holes; but, with the exception of a few tailors and seamstresses, nobody took the slightest interest in what I had provided for their benefit. I am glad that my people are happy, but I cannot restrain a sigh for the failure of my efforts."

"The longer your Majesty lives," said the Stranger, "the better you will understand that we cannot make other people like a thing simply because we like it ourselves."

"Stranger," said the Queen, gazing upon him with admiration, "are you a king in disguise?"

"I am," he replied.

"I thought I perceived it," said the Queen, "and I wish to add that I believe you are far better able to govern this kingdom than I am. If you choose I will resign it to you."

"Not so, your majesty," said the other; "I would not deprive you of your royal position, but I should be happy to share it with you."

"That will answer very well," said the Queen. And turning to an attendant, she gave orders that preparations should be made for their marriage on the following day.

After the royal wedding, which was celebrated with great pomp and grandeur, the Queen paid a visit to the museum, and, much to her surprise, was greatly delighted and interested. The King then informed her that he happened to know where the robbers had stored her collection, which they could not sell or make use of, and if she wished, he would regain the collection and erect a building for its reception.

"We will not do that at present," said the Queen. "When I shall have thoroughly examined and studied all these objects, most of which are entirely new to me, we will decide about the button-holes."

The Hermit's Pupil did not return to his cave. He was greatly delighted with the spice and dash of a robber's life, so different from that of a hermit; and he determined, if possible, to change his business and enter the band. He had a conversation with the Captain on the subject, and that individual encouraged him in his purpose.

"I am tired," the Captain said, "of a robber's life. I have stolen so much, that I cannot use what I have. I take no further interest in accumulating spoils. The quiet of a hermit's life attracts me; and, if you like we will change places. I will become the pupil of your old master, and you shall be the captain of my band."

The change was made. The Captain retired to the cave of the Hermit's Pupil, while the latter, with the hearty consent of all the men, took command of the band of robbers.

When the King heard of this change, he was not at all pleased, and he sent for the ex-pupil.

"I am willing to reward you," he said, "for assisting me in my recent undertaking; but I cannot allow you to lead a band of robbers in my dominions."

A dark shade of disappointment passed over the ex-pupil's features, and his face lengthened visibly.

"It is too bad," he said, "to be thus cut short at the very outset of a brilliant career. I'll tell you what I'll do," he added suddenly, his face brightening, "if you'll let me keep on in my new profession, I'll promise to do nothing but rob robbers."

"Very well," said the King, "if you will confine yourself to that, you may retain your position."

The members of the band were perfectly willing to rob in the new way, for it seemed quite novel and exciting to them. The first place they robbed was their own cave, and as they all had excellent memories, they knew from whom the various goods had been stolen, and every thing was returned to its proper owner. The ex-pupil then led his band against the other dens of robbers in the kingdom, and his movements were conducted with such dash and vigor that the various hordes scattered in every direction, while the treasures in their dens were returned to the owners, or, if these could not be found, were given to the poor. In a short time every robber, except those led by the ex-pupil, had gone into some other business; and the victorious youth led his band into other kingdoms to continue the great work of robbing robbers.

The Queen never sent for the collection of curiosities which the robbers had stolen from her. She was so much interested in the new museum that she continually postponed the re-establishment of her old one; and, as far as can be known, the button-holes are still in the cave where the robbers shut them up.

CHRISTMAS BEFORE LAST;

OR, THE FRUIT OF THE FRAGILE PALM.

THE "Horn o' Plenty" was a fine, big, old-fashioned ship, very high in the bow, very high in the stern, with a quarter-deck always carpeted in fine weather, because her captain could not see why one should not make himself comfortable at sea as well as on land. Covajos Maroots was her captain, and a fine, jolly, old-fashioned, elderly sailor he was. The "Horn o' Plenty" always sailed upon one sea, and always between two ports, one on the west side of the sea, and one on the east. The port on the west was quite a large city, in which Captain Covajos had a married son, and the port on the east was another city in which he had a married daughter. In each family he had several grandchildren; and, consequently, it was a great joy to the jolly old sailor to arrive at either port. The Captain was very particular about his cargo, and the "Horn o' Plenty" was generally laden with good things to eat, or sweet things to smell, or fine things to wear, or beautiful things to look at. Once a merchant brought to him some boxes of bitter aloes, and mustard plasters, but Captain Covajos refused to take them into his ship.

"I know," said he, "that such things are very useful and necessary at times, but you would better send them over in some other vessel. The "Horn o' Plenty" has never carried any thing that to look at, to taste, or to smell, did not delight the souls of old and young. I am sure you cannot say that of these commodities. If I were to put such things on board my ship, it would break the spell which more than fifty savory voyages have thrown around it."

There were sailors who sailed upon that sea who used to say that sometimes, when the weather was hazy and they could not see far, they would know they were about to meet the "Horn o' Plenty" before she came in sight; her planks and timbers, and even her sails and masts, had gradually become so filled with the odor of good things that the winds that blew over her were filled with an agreeable fragrance.

There was another thing about which Captain Covajos was very particular; he always liked to arrive at one of his ports a few days before Christmas. Never, in the course of his long life, had the old sailor spent a Christmas at sea ; and now that he had his fine grandchildren to help make the holidays merry, it would have grieved him very much if he had been unable to reach one or the other of his ports in good season. His jolly old vessel was generally heavily laden, and very slow, and there were many days of calms on that sea when she did not sail at all, so that her voyages were usually very, very long. But the

Captain fixed the days of sailing so as to give himself plenty of time to get to the other end of his course before Christmas came around.

One spring, however, he started too late, and when he was about the middle of his voyage, he called to him Baragat Bean, his old boatswain. This venerable sailor had been with the Captain ever since he had commanded the "Horn o' Plenty," and on important occasions he was always consulted in preference to the other officers, none of whom had served under Captain Covajos more then fifteen or twenty years.

"Baragat," said the Captain, "we have just passed the Isle of Guinea-Hens. You can see its one mountain standing up against the sky to the north."

"Aye, aye, sir," said old Baragat; "there she stands, the same as usual."

"That makes it plain," said the Captain, "that we are not yet half-way across, and I am very much afraid that I shall not be able to reach my dear daughter's house before Christmas."

"That would be doleful, indeed," said Baragat; "but I've feared something of the kind, for we've had calms nearly every other day, and sometimes, when the wind did blow, it came from the wrong direction, and it's my belief that the ship sailed backward."

"That was very bad management," said the Captain. "The chief mate should have seen to it that the sails were turned in such a manner that the ship could not go backward. If that sort of thing happened often, it would become quite a serious affair."

"But what is done can't be helped," said the boatswain, "and I don't see how you are going to get into port before Christmas."

"Nor do I," said the Captain, gazing out over the sea.

"It would give me a sad turn, sir," said Baragat, "to see you spend Christmas at sea; a thing you never did before, nor ever shall do, if I can help it. If you'll take my advice, sir, you'll turn around, and go back. It's a shorter distance to the port we started from than to the one we are going to, and if we turn back now, I am sure we all shall be on shore before the holidays."

"Go back to my son's house!" exclaimed Captain Covajos, "where I was last winter! Why, that would be like spending last Christmas over again!"

"But that would be better than having none at all, sir," said the boatswain, "and a Christmas at sea would be about equal to none."

"Good!" exclaimed the Captain. "I will give up the coming Christmas with my daughter and her children, and go back and spend last Christmas over again with my son and his dear boys and girls. Have the ship turned around immediately, Baragat, and tell the chief mate I do not wish to sail backward if it can possibly be avoided."

For a week or more the "Horn o' Plenty" sailed back upon her track towards the city where dwelt the Captain's son. The weather was fine, the carpet was never taken up from the quarter-deck, and every thing was going on very well, when a man, who happened to have an errand at one of the topmasts, came down, and reported that, far away to the north, he had seen a little open boat with some people in it.

"Ah me!" said Captain Covajos, "it must be some poor fellows who are shipwrecked. It will take us out of our course, but we must not leave them to their fate. Have the ship turned about, so that it will sail northward."

It was not very long before they came up with the boat; and, much to the Captain's surprise, he saw that it was filled with boys.

"Who are you?" he cried as soon as he was near enough. "And where do you come from?"

"We are the First Class in Long Division," said the oldest boy, "and we are cast away. Have you any thing to eat that you can spare us? We are almost famished."

"We have plenty of every thing," said the Captain. "Come on board instantly, and all your wants shall be supplied."

"How long have you been without food?" he asked, when the boys were on the deck of the vessel.

"We have had nothing to eat since breakfast," said one of them; "and it is now late in the afternoon. Some of us are nearly dead from starvation."

"It is very hard for boys to go so long without eating," said the good Captain. And leading them below, he soon set them to work upon a bountiful meal.

Not until their hunger was fully satisfied did he ask them how they came to be cast away.

"You see, sir," said the oldest boy, "that we and

the Multiplication Class had a holiday to-day, and
each class took a boat and determined to have a race,
so as to settle, once for all, which was the highest
branch of arithmetic, multiplication or long division.
Our class rowed so hard that we entirely lost sight of
the Multiplicationers, and found indeed that we were
out of sight of every thing ; so that, at last, we did not
know which was the way back, and thus we became
castaways."

"Where is your school?" asked the Captain.

"It is on Apple Island," said the boy; "and,
although it is a long way off for a small boat with
only four oars for nine boys, it can't be very far for a
ship."

"That is quite likely," said the Captain, "and we
shall take you home. Baragat, tell the chief mate to
have the vessel turned toward Apple Island, that we
may restore these boys to their parents and guardians."

Now, the chief mate had not the least idea in the
world where Apple Island was, but he did not like to
ask, because that would be confessing his ignorance ;
so he steered his vessel toward a point where he be-
lieved he had once seen an island, which, probably,
was the one in question. The "Horn o' Plenty"
sailed in this direction all night, and when day broke,
and there was no island in sight, she took another
course ; and so sailed this way and that for six or
seven days, without ever seeing a sign of land. All
this time, the First Class in Long Division was as
happy as it could be, for it was having a perfect holiday ; fishing off the sides of the vessel, climbing up

the ladders and ropes, and helping the sailors whistle
for wind. But the Captain now began to grow a little
impatient, for he felt he was losing time ; so he sent
for the chief mate, and said to him mildly but firmly:

"I know it is out of the line of your duty to search
for island schools, but, if you really think that you do
not know where Apple Island lies, I wish you to say
so, frankly and openly."

"Frankly and openly," answered the mate, "I
don't think I do."

"Very well," said the Captain. "Now, that is a
basis to work upon, and we know where we stand.
You can take a little rest, and let the second mate find
the island. But I can only give him three days in
which to do it. We really have no time to spare."

The second mate was very proud of the responsibility placed upon him, and immediately ordered the
vessel to be steered due south.

"One is just as likely," he said, "to find a totally
unknown place by going straight ahead in a certain
direction, as by sailing here, there, and everywhere.
In this way, you really get over more water, and there
is less wear and tear of the ship and rigging."

So he sailed due south for two days, and at the end
of that time they came in sight of land. This was
quite a large island, and when they approached near
enough, they saw upon its shores a very handsome
city.

"Is this Apple Island?" said Captain Covajos to
the oldest boy.

"Well, sir," answered the youth, "I am not sure I

can say with certainty that I truly believe that it is; but, I think, if we were to go on shore, the people there would be able to tell us how to go to Apple Island."

"Very likely," said the good Captain; "and we will go on shore and make inquiries. — And it has struck me, Baragat," he said, "that perhaps the merchants in the city where my son lives may be somewhat annoyed when the 'Horn o' Plenty' comes back with all their goods on board, and not disposed of. Not understanding my motives, they may be disposed to think ill of me. Consequently the idea has come into my head, that it might be a good thing to stop here for a time, and try to dispose of some of our merchandise. The city seems to be quite prosperous, and I have no doubt there are a number of merchants here."

So the "Horn o' Plenty" was soon anchored in the harbor, and as many of the officers and crew as could be spared went on shore to make inquiries. Of course the First Class in Long Division was not left behind; and, indeed, they were ashore as soon as anybody. The Captain and his companions were cordially welcomed by some of the dignitaries of the city who had come down to the harbor to see the strange vessel; but no one could give any information in regard to Apple Island, the name of which had never been heard on those shores. The Captain was naturally desirous of knowing at what place he had landed, and was informed that this was the Island of the Fragile Palm.

"That is rather an odd name," said the old Captain. "Why is it so called?"

"The reason is this," said his informant. "Near the centre of the island stands a tall and very slender palm-tree, which has been growing there for hundreds of years. It bears large and handsome fruit which is something like the cocoanut; and, in its perfection, is said to be a transcendently delicious fruit."

"Said to be!" exclaimed the Captain; "are you not positive about it?"

"No," said the other; "no one living has ever tasted the fruit in its perfection. When it becomes overripe, it drops to the ground, and, even then, it is considered royal property, and is taken to the palace for the King's table. But on fête-days and grand occasions small bits of it are distributed to the populace."

"Why don't you pick the fruit," asked Captain Covajos, "when it is in its best condition to eat?"

"It would be impossible," said the citizen, "for any one to climb up that tree, the trunk of which is so extremely delicate and fragile that the weight of a man would probably snap it; and, of course, a ladder placed against it would produce the same result. Many attempts have been made to secure this fruit at the proper season, but all of them have failed. Another palm-tree of a more robust sort was once planted near this one in the hope that when it grew high enough, men could climb up the stronger tree and get the fruit from the other. But, although we waited many years the second tree never attained sufficient height, and it was cut down."

"It is a great pity," said the Captain; "but I

suppose it cannot be helped." And then he began to make inquiries about the merchants in the place, and what probability there was of his doing a little trade here. The Captain soon discovered that the cargo of his ship was made up of goods which were greatly desired by the citizens of this place; and for several days he was very busy in selling the good things to eat, the sweet things to smell, the fine things to wear, and the beautiful things to look at, with which the hold of the "Horn o' Plenty" was crowded.

During this time the First Class in Long Division roamed, in delight, over the city. The busy streets, the shops, the handsome buildings, and the queer sights which they occasionally met, interested and amused them greatly. But still the boys were not satisfied. They had heard of the Fragile Palm, and they made up their minds to go and have a look at it. Therefore, taking a guide, they tramped out into the country, and in about an hour they came in sight of the beautiful tree standing in the centre of the plain. The trunk was, indeed, exceedingly slender, and, as the guide informed them, the wood was of so very brittle a nature that if the tree had not been protected from the winds by the high hills which encircled it, it would have been snapped off ages ago. Under the broad tuft of leaves that formed its top, the boys saw hanging large clusters of the precious fruit; great nuts as big as their heads.

"At what time of the year," asked the oldest boy, "is that fruit just ripe enough to eat?"

"Now," answered the guide. "This is the season

when it is in the most perfect condition. In about a month it will become entirely too ripe and soft, and will drop. But, even then, the King and all the rest of us are glad enough to get a taste of it."

"I should think the King would be exceedingly eager to get some of it, just as it is," said the boy.

"Indeed he is!" replied the guide. "He and his father, and I don't know how many grandfathers back, have offered large rewards to any one who would procure them this fruit in its best condition. But nobody has ever been able to get any yet."

"The reward still holds good, I suppose," said the head boy.

"Oh, yes," answered the guide; "there never was a King who so much desired to taste the fruit as our present monarch."

The oldest boy looked up at the top of the tree, shut one eye, and gave his head a little wag. Whereupon every boy in the class looked up, shut one eye, and slightly wagged his head. After which the oldest boy said that he thought it was about time for them to go back to the ship.

As soon as they reached the vessel, and could talk together freely, the boys had an animated discussion. It was unanimously agreed that they would make an attempt to get some of the precious fruit from the Fragile Palm, and the only difference of opinion among them was as to how it should be done Most of them were in favor of some method of climbing the tree and trusting to its not breaking. But this the oldest boy would not listen to ; the trunk might snap, and then somebody would be hurt, and he felt, in a measure, responsible for the rest of the class. At length a good plan was proposed by a boy who had studied mechanics.

"What we ought to do with that tree," said he, "is to put a hinge into her. Then we could let her down gently, pick off the fruit, and set her up again.

"But how are you going to do it?" asked the others.

"This is the way," said the boy who had studied mechanics. "You take a saw, and then, about two feet from the ground, you begin and saw down diagonally, for a foot and a half, to the centre of the trunk. Then you go on the other side, and saw down in the same way, the two cuts meeting each other. Now you have the upper part of the trunk ending in a wedge, which fits into a cleft in the lower part of the trunk. Then, about nine inches below the place where you first began to saw, you bore a hole straight through both sides of the cleft and the wedge between them. Then you put an iron bolt through this hole, and you have your tree on a hinge, only she wont be apt to move because she fits in so snug and tight. Then you get a long rope, and put one end in a slip-knot loosely around the trunk. Then you get a lot of poles, and tie them end to end, and push this slip-knot up until it is somewhere near the top, when you pull it tight. Then you take another rope with a slip-knot, and push this a little more than half-way up the trunk. By having two ropes, that way, you prevent too much strain coming on any one part of the trunk.

Then, after that, you take a mallet and chisel and round off the lower corners of the wedge, so that it will turn easily in the cleft. Then we take hold of the ropes, let her down gently, pick off the fruit, and haul her up again. That will all be easy enough.''

This plan delighted the boys, and they all pronounced in its favor; but the oldest one suggested that it would be better to fasten the ropes to the trunk before they began to saw upon it, and another boy asked how they were going to keep the tree standing when they hauled her up again.

''Oh, that is easy,'' said the one who had studied mechanics; ''you just bore another hole about six inches above the first one, and put in another bolt. Then, of course, she can't move.''

This settled all the difficulties, and it was agreed to start out early the next morning, gather the fruit, and claim the reward the King had offered. They accordingly went to the Captain and asked him for a sharp saw, a mallet and chisel, an auger, two iron bolts, and two very long ropes. These, having been cheerfully given to them, were put away in readiness for the work to be attempted.

Very early on the next morning, the First Class in Long Division set out for the Fragile Palm, carrying their tools and ropes. Few people were awake as they passed through the city, and, without being observed, they reached the little plain on which the tree stood. The ropes were attached at the proper places, the tree was sawn, diagonally, according to the plan; the bolt was put in, and the corners of the wedge were rounded off. Then the eldest boy produced a pound of butter, whereupon his comrades, who had seized the ropes, paused in surprise and asked him why he had brought the butter.

" I thought it well," was the reply, " to bring along some butter, because, when the tree is down, we can grease the hinge, and then it will not be so hard to pull it up again."

When all was ready, eight of the boys took hold of the long ropes, while another one with a pole pushed against the trunk of the Fragile Palm. When it began to lean over a little, he dropped his pole and ran to help the others with the ropes. Slowly the tree moved on its hinge, descending at first very gradually ; but it soon began to move with greater rapidity, although the boys held it back with all their strength ; and, in spite of their most desperate efforts, the top came to the ground at last with a great thump. And then they all dropped their ropes, and ran for the fruit. Fortunately the great nuts incased in their strong husks were not in the least injured, and the boys soon pulled them off, about forty in all. Some of the boys were in favor of cracking open a few of the nuts and eating them, but this the eldest boy positively forbade.

" This fruit," he said, " is looked upon as almost sacred, and if we were to eat any of it, it is probable that we should be put to death, which would be extremely awkward for fellows who have gone to all the trouble we have had. We must set up the tree and carry the fruit to the King."

According to this advice, they thoroughly greased the hinge in the tree with the butter, and then set themselves to work to haul up the trunk. This, however, was much more difficult than letting it down; and they had to lift up the head of it, and prop it up on poles, before they could pull upon it with advantage. The tree, although tall, was indeed a very slender one, with a small top, and, if it had been as fragile as it was supposed to be, the boys' efforts would surely have broken it. At last, after much tugging and warm work, they pulled it into an upright position, and put in the second bolt. They left the ropes on the tree because, as some of them had suggested, the people might want to let the tree down again the next year. It would have been difficult for the boys to carry in their arms the great pile of fruit they had gathered; but, having noticed a basket-maker's cottage on their way to the tree, two of them were sent to buy one of his largest baskets or hampers. This was attached to two long poles, and, having been filled with the nuts, the boys took the poles on their shoulders, and marched into the city.

On their way to the palace they attracted a great crowd, and when they were ushered into the presence of the King, his surprise and delight knew no bounds. At first he could scarcely believe his eyes; but he had seen the fruit so often that there could be no mistake about it.

"I shall not ask you," he said to the boys, "how you procured this fruit, and thus accomplished a deed which has been the object of the ambition of myself and my forefathers. All I ask is, did you leave the tree standing?"

"We did," said the boys.

"Then all that remains to be done," said His Majesty, "is to give you the reward you have so nobly earned. Treasurer, measure out to each of them a quart of gold coin. And pray be quick about it, for I am wild with desire to have a table spread, and one of these nuts cracked, that I may taste of its luscious contents."

The boys, however, appeared a little dissatisfied. Huddling together, they consulted in a low tone, and then the eldest boy addressed the King.

"May it please your Majesty," he said; "we should very much prefer to have you give each of us one of those nuts instead of a quart of gold."

The King looked grave. "This is a much greater reward," he said, "than I had ever expected to pay; but, since you ask it, you must have it. You have done something which none of my subjects has ever been able to accomplish, and it is right, therefore, that you should be fully satisfied."

So he gave them each a nut, with which they departed in triumph to the ship.

By the afternoon of the next day, the Captain had sold all his cargo at very good prices; and when the money was safely stored away in the "Horn o' Plenty," he made ready to sail, for he declared he had really no time to spare. "I must now make all possible haste," he said to old Baragat, "to find Apple Island, put these boys ashore, and then speed away to the city where lives my son. We must not fail to get there in time to spend last Christmas over again.''

On the second day, after the '' Horn o' Plenty '' had left the Island of the Fragile Palm, one of the sailors who happened to be aloft noticed a low, black, and exceedingly unpleasant-looking vessel rapidly approaching. This soon proved to be the ship of a band of corsairs, who, having heard of the large amount of money on the '' Horn o' Plenty,'' had determined to pursue her and capture the rich prize. All sails were set upon the '' Horn o' Plenty,'' but it soon became plain that she could never outsail the corsair vessel.

'' What our ship can do better than any thing else,'' said Baragat to the Captain, '' is to stop short. Stop her short, and let the other one go by.''

This manœuvre was executed, but, although the corsair passed rapidly by, not being able to stop so suddenly, it soon turned around and came back, its decks swarming with savage men armed to the teeth.

'' They are going to board us,'' cried Baragat. '' They are getting out their grappling-irons, and they will fasten the two ships together.''

'' Let all assemble on the quarter-deck,'' said the Captain. '' It is higher there, and we shall not be so much exposed to accidents.''

The corsair ship soon ran alongside the '' Horn o' Plenty,'' and in a moment the two vessels were fastened together ; and then the corsairs, every man of them, each with cutlass in hand and a belt full of dirks and knives, swarmed up the side of the '' Horn o' Plenty,'' and sprang upon its central deck. Some of the ferocious fellows, seeing the officers and crew all huddled together upon the quarter-deck, made a movement in that direction. This so frightened the chief mate that he sprang down upon the deck of the corsair ship. A panic now arose, and he was immediately followed by the officers and crew. The boys, of course, were not to be left behind; and the Captain and Baragat felt themselves bound not to desert the crew, and so they jumped also. None of the corsairs interfered with this proceeding, for each one of them was anxious to find the money at once. When the passengers and crew of the "Horn o' Plenty" were all on board the corsair ship, Baragat came to the Captain, and said:

"If I were you, sir, I'd cast off those grapnels, and separate the vessels. If we don't do that those rascals, when they have finished robbing our money-chests, will come back here and murder us all."

"That is a good idea," said Captain Covajos; and he told the chief mate to give orders to cast off the grapnels, push the two vessels apart, and set some of the sails.

When this had been done, the corsair vessel began to move away from the other, and was soon many lengths distant from her. When the corsairs came on deck and perceived what had happened, they were infuriated, and immediately began to pursue their own vessel with the one they had captured. But the "Horn o' Plenty" could not, by any possibility, sail as fast as the corsair ship, and the latter easily kept away from her.

" Now, then," said Baragat to the Captain, "what you have to do is easy enough. Sail straight for our port and those sea-robbers will follow you; for, of course, they will wish to get their own vessel back again, and will hope, by some carelessness on our part, to overtake us. In the mean time the money will be safe enough, for they will have no opportunity of spending it; and when we come to port, we can take some soldiers on board, and go back and capture those fellows. They can never sail away from us on the " Horn o' Plenty."

" That is an admirable plan," said the Captain, " and I shall carry it out; but I cannot sail to port immediately. I must first find Apple Island and land these boys, whose parents and guardians are probably growing very uneasy. I suppose the corsairs will continue to follow us wherever we go."

" I hope so," said Baragat; "at any rate we shall see."

The First Class in Long Division was very much delighted with the change of vessels, and the boys rambled everywhere, and examined with great interest all that belonged to the corsairs. They felt quite easy about the only treasures they possessed, because, when they had first seen the piratical vessel approaching, they had taken the precious nuts which had been given to them by the King, and had hidden them at the bottom of some large boxes, in which the Captain kept the sailors' winter clothes.

" In this warm climate," said the eldest boy, " the robbers will never meddle with those winter clothes, and our precious fruit will be perfectly safe."

"If you had taken my advice," said one of the other boys, "we should have eaten some of the nuts. Those, at least, we should have been sure of."

"And we should have had that many less to show to the other classes," said the eldest boy. "Nuts like these, I am told, if picked at the proper season, will keep for a long time."

For some days the corsairs on board the "Horn of Plenty" followed their own vessel, but then they seemed to despair of ever being able to overtake it, and steered in another direction. This threatened to ruin all the plans of Captain Covajos, and his mind became troubled. Then the boy who had studied mechanics came forward and said to the Captain:

"I'll tell you what I'd do, sir, if I were you; I'd follow your old ship, and when night came on I'd sail up quite near to her, and let some of your sailors swim quietly over, and fasten a cable to her, and then you could tow her after you wherever you wished to go."

"But they might unfasten the cable, or cut it," said Baragat, who was standing by.

"That could easily be prevented," said the boy. "At their end of the cable must be a stout chain which they cannot cut, and it must be fastened so far beneath the surface of the water that they will not be able to reach it to unfasten it."

"A most excellent plan," said Captain Covajos; "let it be carried out."

As soon as it became quite dark, the corsair vessel

quietly approached the other, and two stout sailors from Finland, who swam very well, were ordered to swim over and attach the chain-end of a long cable to the "Horn o' Plenty." It was a very difficult operation, for the chain was heavy, but the men succeeded at last, and returned to report.

"We put the chain on, fast and strong sir," they said to the Captain; "and six feet under water. But the only place we could find to make it fast to was the bottom of the rudder."

"That will do very well," remarked Baragat; "for the 'Horn o' Plenty' sails better backward than forward, and will not be so hard to tow."

For week after week, and month after month, Captain Covajos, in the corsair vessel, sailed here and there in search of Apple Island, always towing after him the "Horn o' Plenty," with the corsairs on board, but never an island with a school on it could they find; and one day old Baragat came to the Captain and said:

"If I were you, sir, I'd sail no more in these warm regions. I am quite sure that apples grow in colder latitudes, and are never found so far south as this."

"That is a good idea," said Captain Covajos. "We should sail for the north if we wished to find an island of apples. Have the vessel turned northward."

And so, for days and weeks, the two vessels slowly moved on to the north. One day the Captain made some observations and calculations, and then he hastily summoned Baragat.

"Do you know," said he, "that I find it is now

near the end of November, and I am quite certain that we shall not get to the port where my son lives in time to celebrate last Christmas again. It is dreadfully slow work, towing after us the 'Horn o' Plenty,' full of corsairs, wherever we go. But we cannot cast her off and sail straight for our port, for I should lose my good ship, the merchants would lose all their money, and the corsairs would go unpunished; and, besides all that, think of the misery of the parents and guardians of those poor boys. No; I must endeavor to find Apple Island. And if I cannot reach port in time to spend last Christmas with my son, I shall certainly get there in season for Christmas before last. It is true that I spent that Christmas with my daughter, but I cannot go on to her now. I am much nearer the city where my son lives; and, besides, it is necessary to go back, and give the merchants their money. So now we shall have plenty of time, and need not feel hurried.''

"No," said Baragat, heaving a vast sigh, "we need not feel hurried."

The mind of the eldest boy now became very much troubled, and he called his companions about him. "I don't like at all," said he, "this sailing to the north. It is now November, and, although it is warm enough at this season in the southern part of the sea, it will become colder and colder as we go on. The consequence of this will be that those corsairs will want winter clothes, they will take them out of the Captain's chests, and they will find our fruit."

The boys groaned. "That is true," said one of

them; "but still we wish to go back to our island."

"Of course," said the eldest boy, "it is quite proper that we should return to Long Division. But think of the hard work we did to get that fruit, and think of the quarts of gold we gave up for it! It would be too bad to lose it now!"

It was unanimously agreed that it would be too bad to lose the fruit, and it was also unanimously agreed that they wished to go back to Apple Island. But what to do about it, they did not know.

Day by day the weather grew colder and colder, and the boys became more and more excited and distressed for fear they should lose their precious fruit. The eldest boy lay awake for several nights, and then a plan came into his head. He went to Captain Covajos and proposed that he should send a flag of truce over to the corsairs, offering to exchange winter clothing. He would send over to them the heavy garments they had left on their own vessel, and in return would take the boxes of clothes intended for the winter wear of his sailors. In this way, they would get their fruit back without the corsairs knowing any thing about it. The Captain considered this an excellent plan, and ordered the chief mate to take a boat and a flag of truce, and go over to the "Horn o' Plenty," and make the proposition. The eldest boy and two of the others insisted on going also, in order that there might be no mistake about the boxes. But when the flag-of-truce party reached the "Horn o' Plenty" they found not a corsair there! Every man of them had gone. They had taken with them all the money-chests, but to the great delight of the boys, the boxes of winter clothes had not been disturbed; and in them still nestled, safe and sound, the precious nuts of the Fragile Palm.

When the matter had been thoroughly looked into, it became quite evident what the corsairs had done. There had been only one boat on board the "Horn o' Plenty," and that was the one on which the First Class in Long Division had arrived. The night before, the two vessels had passed within a mile or so of a large island, which the Captain had approached in the hope it was the one they were looking for, and they passed it so slowly that the corsairs had time to ferry themselves over, a few at a time, in the little boat, taking with them the money, — and all without discovery.

Captain Covajos was greatly depressed when he heard of the loss of all the money.

"I shall have a sad tale to tell my merchants," he said, "and Christmas before last will not be celebrated so joyously as it was the first time. But we cannot help what has happened, and we all must endeavor to bear our losses with patience. We shall continue our search for Apple Island, but I shall go on board my own ship, for I have greatly missed my carpeted quarter-deck and my other comforts. The chief mate, however, and a majority of the crew shall remain on board the corsair vessel, and continue to tow us. The 'Horn o' Plenty' sails better stern foremost, and we shall go faster that way."

The boys were overjoyed at recovering their fruit, and most of them were in favor of cracking two or three of the great nuts, and eating their contents in honor of the occasion, but the eldest boy dissuaded them.

"The good Captain," he said, "has been very kind in endeavoring to take us back to our school, and still intends to keep up the search for dear old Apple Island. The least we can do for him is to give him this fruit, which is all we have, and let him do what he pleases with it. This is the only way in which we can show our gratitude to him."

The boys turned their backs on one another, and each of them gave his eyes a little rub, but they all agreed to give the fruit to the Captain.

When the good old man received his present, he was much affected. "I will accept what you offer me," he said ; "for if I did not, I know your feelings would be wounded. But you must keep one of the nuts for yourselves. And, more than that, if we do not find Apple Island in the course of the coming year, I invite you all to spend Christmas before last over again, with me at my son's house."

All that winter, the two ships sailed up and down, and here and there, but never could they find Apple Island. When Christmas-time came, old Baragat went around among the boys and the crew, and told them it would be well not to say a word on the subject to the Captain, for his feelings were very tender in regard to spending Christmas away from his families, and the thing had never happened before. So nobody made any allusion to the holidays, and they passed over as if they had been ordinary days.

During the spring, and all through the summer, the two ships kept up the unavailing search, but when the autumn began, Captain Covajos said to old Baragat: "I am very sorry, but I feel that I can no longer look for Apple Island. I must go back and spend Christmas before last over again, with my dearest son ; and if these poor boys never return to their homes, I am sure they cannot say it was any fault of mine."

"No, sir," said Baragat, "I think you have done all that could be expected of you."

So the ships sailed to the city on the west side of the sea ; and the Captain was received with great joy by his son, and his grandchildren. He went to the merchants, and told them how he had lost all their money. He hoped they would be able to bear their misfortune with fortitude, and begged, as he could do nothing else for them, that they would accept the eight great nuts from the Fragile Palm that the boys had given him. To his surprise the merchants became wild with delight when they received the nuts. The money they had lost was as nothing, they said, compared to the value of this incomparable and precious fruit, picked in its prime, and still in a perfect condition.

It had been many, many generations since this rare fruit, the value of which was like unto that of diamonds and pearls, had been for sale in any market in the world ; and kings and queens in many countries were ready to give for it almost any price that might be asked.

When the good old Captain heard this he was greatly rejoiced, and, as the holidays were now near, he insisted that the boys should spend Christmas before last over again, at his son's house. He found that a good many people here knew where Apple Island was, and he made arrangements for the First Class in Long Division to return to that island in a vessel which was to sail about the first of the year.

The boys still possessed the great nut which the Captain had insisted they should keep for themselves, and he now told them that if they chose to sell it, they would each have a nice little fortune to take back with them. The eldest boy consulted the others, and then he said to the Captain :

"Our class has gone through a good many hardships, and has had a lot of trouble with that palm-tree and other things, and we think we ought to be rewarded. So, if it is all the same to you, I think we will crack the nut on Christmas Day and we all will eat it."

"I never imagined," cried Captain Covajos, as he sat, on that Christmas Day, surrounded by his son's family and the First Class in Long Division, the eyes of the whole party sparkling with ecstasy as they tasted the peerless fruit of the Fragile Palm, "that Christmas before last could be so joyfully celebrated over again."

PRINCE HASSAK'S MARCH.

IN the spring of a certain year, long since passed away, Prince Hassak, of Itoby, determined to visit his uncle, the King of Yan.

"Whenever my uncle visited us," said the Prince, "or when my late father went to see him, the journey was always made by sea; and, in order to do this, it was necessary to go in a very roundabout way between Itoby and Yan. Now, I shall do nothing of this kind. It is beneath the dignity of a prince to go out of his way on account of capes, peninsulas, and promontories. I shall march from my palace to that of my uncle in a straight line. I shall go across the country, and no obstacle shall cause me to deviate from my course. Mountains and hills shall be tunnelled, rivers shall be bridged, houses shall be levelled; a road shall be cut through forests; and, when I have finished my march, the course over which I have passed shall be a mathematically straight line. Thus will I show to the world that, when a prince desires to travel, it is not necessary for him to go out of his way on account of obstacles."

As soon as possible after the Prince had determined

upon this march, he made his preparations, and set out. He took with him a few courtiers, and a large body of miners, rock-splitters, bridge-builders, and workmen of that class, whose services would, very probably, be needed. Besides these, he had an officer whose duty it was to point out the direct course to be taken, and another who was to draw a map of the march, showing the towns, mountains, and the various places it passed through. There were no compasses in those days, but the course-marker had an instrument which he would set in a proper direction by means of the stars, and then he could march by it all day. Besides these persons, Prince Hassak selected from the schools of his city five boys and five girls, and took them with him. He wished to show them how, when a thing was to be done, the best way was to go straight ahead and do it, turning aside for nothing.

"When they grow up they will teach these things to their children," said he; "and thus I shall instil good principles into my people."

The first day Prince Hassak and his party marched over a level country, with no further trouble than that occasioned by the tearing down of fences and walls, and the destruction of a few cottages and barns. After encamping for the night, they set out the next morning, but had not marched many miles before they came to a rocky hill, on the top of which was a handsome house, inhabited by a Jolly-cum-pop.

"Your Highness," said the course-marker, "in order to go in a direct line we must make a tunnel through this hill, immediately under the house. This may cause the building to fall in, but the rubbish can be easily removed."

"Let the men go to work," said the Prince. "I will dismount from my horse, and watch the proceedings."

When the Jolly-cum-pop saw the party halt before his house, he hurried out to pay his respects to the Prince. When he was informed of what was to be done, the Jolly-cum-pop could not refrain from laughing aloud.

"I never heard," he said, "of such a capital idea. It is so odd and original. It will be very funny, I am sure, to see a tunnel cut right under my house."

The miners and rock-splitters now began to work at the base of the hill, and then the Jolly-cum-pop made a proposition to the Prince.

"It will take your men some time," he said, "to cut this tunnel, and it is a pity your Highness should not be amused in the meanwhile. It is a fine day: suppose we go into the forest and hunt."

This suited the Prince very well, for he did not care about sitting under a tree and watching his workmen, and the Jolly-cum-pop having sent for his horse and some bows and arrows, the whole party, with the exception of the laborers, rode toward the forest, a short distance away.

"What shall we find to hunt?" asked the Prince of the Jolly-cum-pop.

"I really do not know," exclaimed the latter, " but we'll hunt whatever we happen to see — deer, small birds, rabbits, griffins, rhinoceroses, any thing that comes along. I feel as gay as a skipping grasshopper. My spirits rise like a soaring bird. What a joyful thing it is to have such a hunt on such a glorious day!"

The gay and happy spirits of the Jolly-cum-pop affected the whole party, and they rode merrily through the forest; but they found no game; and, after an hour or two, they emerged into the open country again. At a distance, on a slight elevation, stood a large and massive building.

"I am hungry and thirsty," said the Prince, "and perhaps we can get some refreshments at yonder house. So far, this has not been a very fine hunt."

"No," cried the Jolly-cum-pop, "not yet. But what a joyful thing to see a hospitable mansion just at the moment when we begin to feel a little tired and hungry!"

The building they were approaching belonged to a Potentate, who lived at a great distance. In some of his travels he had seen this massive house, and thought it would make a good prison. He accordingly bought it, fitted it up as a jail, and appointed a jailer and three myrmidons to take charge of it. This had occurred years before, but no prisoners had ever been sent to this jail. A few days preceding the Jolly-cum-pop's hunt, the Potentate had journeyed this way and had stopped at his jail. After inquiring into its condition, he had said to the jailer:

"It is now fourteen years since I appointed you to this place, and in all that time there have been no prisoners, and you and your men have been drawing

your wages without doing any thing. I shall return
this way in a few days, and if I still find you idle I
shall discharge you all and close the jail.''

This filled the jailer with great dismay, for he did
not wish to lose his good situation. When he saw the
Prince and his party approaching, the thought struck
him that perhaps he might make prisoners of them,
and so not be found idle when the Potentate returned.
He came out to meet the hunters, and when they asked
if they could here find refreshment, he gave them a
most cordial welcome. His men took their horses,
and, inviting them to enter, he showed each member
of the party into a small bedroom, of which there
seemed to be a great many.

'' Here are water and towels,'' he said to each one,
'' and when you have washed your face and hands,
your refreshments will be ready.'' Then, going out,
he locked the door on the outside.

The party numbered seventeen: the Prince, three
courtiers, five boys, five girls, the course-marker, the
map-maker, and the Jolly-cum-pop. The heart of the
jailer was joyful; seventeen inmates was something to
be proud of. He ordered his myrmidons to give the
prisoners a meal of bread and water through the holes
in their cell-doors, and then he sat down to make out
his report to the Potentate.

'' They must all be guilty of crimes,'' he said to
himself, '' which are punished by long imprisonment.
I don't want any of them executed.''

So he numbered his prisoners from one to seventeen,
according to the cell each happened to be in, and he

wrote a crime opposite each number. The first was highway robbery, the next forgery, and after that followed treason, smuggling, barn-burning, bribery, poaching, usury, piracy, witchcraft, assault and battery, using false weights and measures, burglary, counterfeiting, robbing hen-roosts, conspiracy, and poisoning his grandmother by proxy.

This report was scarcely finished when the Potentate returned. He was very much surprised to find that seventeen prisoners had come in since his previous visit, and he read the report with interest.

"Here is one who ought to be executed," he said, referring to Number Seventeen. "And how did he poison his grandmother by proxy? Did he get another woman to be poisoned in her stead? Or did he employ some one to act in his place as the poisoner?"

"I have not yet been fully informed, my lord," said the jailer, fearful that he should lose a prisoner; "but this is his first offence, and his grandmother, who did not die, has testified to his general good character."

"Very well," said the Potentate; "but if he ever does it again, let him be executed; and, by the way, I should like to see the prisoners."

Thereupon the jailer conducted the Potentate along the corridors, and let him look through the holes in the doors at the prisoners within.

"What is this little girl in for?" he asked.

The jailer looked at the number over the door, and then at his report.

"Piracy," he answered.

"A strange offence for such a child," said the Potentate.

"They often begin that sort of thing very early in life," said the jailer.

"And this fine gentleman," said the Potentate, looking in at the Prince, "what did he do?"

The jailer glanced at the number, and the report.

"Robbed hen-roosts," he said.

"He must have done a good deal of it to afford to dress so well," said the Potentate, passing on, and looking into other cells. "It seems to me that many of your prisoners are very young."

"It is best to take them young, my lord," said the jailer. "They are very hard to catch when they grow up."

The Potentate then looked in at the Jolly-cum-pop, and asked what was his offence.

"Conspiracy," was the answer.

"And where are the other conspirators?"

"There was only one," said the jailer.

Number Seventeen was the oldest of the courtiers.

"He appears to be an elderly man to have a grandmother," said the Potentate. "She must be very aged, and that makes it all the worse for him. I think he should be executed."

"Oh, no, my lord," cried the jailer. "I am assured that his crime was quite unintentional."

"Then he should be set free," said the Potentate.

"I mean to say," said the jailer, "that it was just enough intentional to cause him to be imprisoned here for a long time, but not enough to deserve execution."

" Very well," said the Potentate, turning to leave ; " take good care of your prisoners, and send me a report every month."

" That will I do, my lord," said the jailer, bowing very low.

The Prince and his party had been very much surprised and incensed when they found that they could not get out of their rooms, and they had kicked and banged and shouted until they were tired, but the jailer had informed them that they were to be confined there for years ; and when the Potentate arrived they had resigned themselves to despair. The Jolly-cum-pop, however, was affected in a different way. It seemed to him the most amusing joke in the world that a person should deliberately walk into a prison-cell and be locked up for several years ; and he lay down on his little bed and laughed himself to sleep.

That night one of the boys sat at his iron-barred window, wide awake. He was a Truant, and had never yet been in any place from which he could not run away. He felt that his school-fellows depended upon him to run away and bring them assistance, and he knew that his reputation as a Truant was at stake. His responsibility was so heavy that he could not sleep, and he sat at the window, trying to think of a way to get out. After some hours the moon arose, and by its light he saw upon the grass, not far from his window, a number of little creatures, which at first he took for birds or small squirrels ; but on looking more attentively he perceived that they were pigwidgeons. They were standing around a flat stone, and seemed to be

making calculations on it with a piece of chalk. At
this sight, the heart of the Truant jumped for joy.
"Pigwidgeons can do any thing," he said to himself,
"and these certainly can get us out." He now tried
in various ways to attract the attention of the pigwidgeons; but as he was afraid to call or whistle very
loud, for fear of arousing the jailor, he did not succeed.
Happily, he thought of a pea-shooter which he had in
his pocket, and taking this out he blew a pea into the
midst of the little group with such force that it knocked
the chalk from the hand of the pigwidgeon who was
using it. The little fellows looked up in astonishment,
and perceived the Truant beckoning to them from his
window. At first they stood angrily regarding him;
but on his urging them in a loud whisper to come to
his relief, they approached the prison and, clambering
up a vine, soon reached his window-sill. The Truant
now told his mournful tale, to which the pigwidgeons
listened very attentively; and then, after a little con-
sultation among themselves, one of them said: "We
will get you out if you will tell us how to divide five-
sevenths by six."

The poor Truant was silent for an instant, and then
he said: "That is not the kind of thing I am good
at, but I expect some of the other fellows could tell
you easily enough. Our windows must be all in a row,
and you can climb up and ask some of them; and if
any one tells you, will you get us all out?"

"Yes," said the pigwidgeon who had spoken before.
"We will do that, for we are very anxious to know
how to divide five-sevenths by six. We have been

working at it for four or five days, and there wont be any thing worth dividing if we wait much longer."

The pigwidgeons now began to descend the vine; but one of them lingering a little, the Truant, who had a great deal of curiosity, asked him what it was they had to divide.

"There were eight of us," the pigwidgeon answered, "who helped a farmer's wife, and she gave us a pound of butter. She did not count us properly, and divided the butter into seven parts. We did not notice this at first, and two of the party, who were obliged to go away to a distance, took their portions and departed, and now we can not divide among six the five-sevenths that remain."

"That is a pretty hard thing," said the Truant, "but I am sure some of the boys can tell you how to do it."

The pigwidgeons visited the next four cells, which were occupied by four boys, but not one of them could tell how to divide five-sevenths by six. The Prince was questioned, but he did not know; and neither did the course-marker, nor the map-maker. It was not until they came to the cell of the oldest girl that they received an answer. She was good at mental arithmetic; and, after a minute's thought, she said, "It would be five forty-seconds."

"Good!" cried the pigwidgeons. "We will divide the butter into forty-two parts, and each take five. And now let us go to work and cut these bars."

Three of the six pigwidgeons were workers in iron, and they had their little files and saws in pouches by their sides. They went to work manfully, and the others helped them, and before morning one bar was cut in each of the seventeen windows. The cells were all on the ground floor, and it was quite easy for the prisoners to clamber out. That is, it was easy for all but the Jolly-cum-pop. He had laughed so much in his life that he had grown quite fat, and he found it impossible to squeeze himself through the opening made by the removal of one iron bar. The sixteen other prisoners had all departed; the pigwidgeons had hurried away to divide their butter into forty-two parts, and the Jolly-cum-pop still remained in his cell, convulsed with laughter at the idea of being caught in such a curious predicament.

"It is the most ridiculous thing in the world," he said. "I suppose I must stay here and cry until I get thin." And the idea so tickled him, that he laughed himself to sleep.

The Prince and his party kept together, and hurried from the prison as fast as they could. When the day broke they had gone several miles, and then they stopped to rest. "Where is that Jolly-cum-pop?" said the Prince. "I suppose he has gone home. He is a pretty fellow to lead us into this trouble and then desert us! How are we to find the way back to his house? Course-marker, can you tell us the direction in which we should go?"

"Not until to-night, your Highness," answered the course-marker, "when I can set my instrument by the stars."

The Prince's party was now in a doleful plight.

Every one was very hungry; they were in an open plain, no house was visible, and they knew not which way to go. They wandered about for some time, looking for a brook or a spring where they might quench their thirst; and then a rabbit sprang out from some bushes. The whole party immediately started off in pursuit of the rabbit. They chased it here, there, backward and forward, through hollows and over hills, until it ran quite away and disappeared. Then they were more tired, thirsty, and hungry than before; and, to add to their miseries, when night came on the sky was cloudy, and the course-marker could not set his instrument by the stars. It would be difficult to find sixteen more miserable people than the Prince and his companions when they awoke the next morning from their troubled sleep on the hard ground. Nearly starved, they gazed at one another with feelings of despair.

"I feel," said the Prince, in a weak voice, "that there is nothing I would not do to obtain food. I would willingly become a slave if my master would give me a good breakfast."

"So would I," ejaculated each of the others.

About an hour after this, as they were all sitting disconsolately upon the ground, they saw, slowly approaching, a large cart drawn by a pair of oxen. On the front of the cart, which seemed to be heavily loaded, sat a man, with a red beard, reading a book. The boys, when they saw the cart, set up a feeble shout, and the man, lifting his eyes from his book, drove directly toward the group on the ground. Dismounting, he approached Prince Hassak, who immediately told him his troubles and implored relief. "We will do any thing," said the Prince, "to obtain food."

Standing for a minute in a reflective mood, the man with the red beard addressed the Prince in a slow, meditative manner: "How would you like," he said, "to form a nucleus?"

"Can we get any thing to eat by it?" eagerly asked the Prince.

"Yes," replied the man, "you can."

"We'll do it!" immediately cried the whole sixteen, without waiting for further information.

"Which will you do first," said the man, "listen to my explanations, or eat?"

"Eat!" cried the entire sixteen in chorus.

The man now produced from his cart a quantity of bread, meat, wine, and other provisions, which he distributed generously, but judiciously, to the hungry Prince and his followers. Every one had enough, but no one too much. And soon, revived and strengthened, they felt like new beings.

"Now," said the Prince, "we are ready to form a nucleus, as we promised. How is it done?"

"I will explain the matter to you in a few words," said the man with the red beard. "For a long time I have been desirous to found a city. In order to do this one must begin by forming a nucleus. Every great city is started from a nucleus. A few persons settle down in some particular spot, and live there. Then they are a nucleus. Then other people come there, and gather around this nucleus, and then more

people come and more, until in course of time there
is a great city. I have loaded this cart with provisions, tools, and other things that are necessary for
my purpose, and have set out to find some people who
would be willing to form a nucleus. I am very glad
to have found you and that you are willing to enter
into my plan; and this seems a good spot for us to
settle upon.''

"What is the first thing to be done?" said the
Prince.

"We must all go to work," said the man with the
red beard, "to build dwellings, and also a school-house
for these young people. Then we must till some
ground in the suburbs, and lay the foundations, at
least, of a few public buildings.''

"All this will take a good while, will it not?" said
the Prince.

"Yes," said the man, "it will take a good while;
and the sooner we set about it, the better.''

Thereupon tools were distributed among the party,
and Prince, courtiers, boys, girls, and all went to work
to build houses and form the nucleus of a city.

When the jailer looked into his cells in the morning,
and found that all but one of his prisoners had escaped,
he was utterly astounded, and his face, when the Jolly-
cum-pop saw him, made that individual roar with
laughter. The jailer, however, was a man accustomed to deal with emergencies. "You need not
laugh," he said, "every thing shall go on as before,
and I shall take no notice of the absence of your companions. You are now numbered One to Seventee

inclusive, and you stand charged with highway robbery, forgery, treason, smuggling, barn-burning, bribery, poaching, usury, piracy, witchcraft, assault and battery, using false weights and measures, burglary, counterfeiting, robbing hen-roosts, conspiracy, and poisoning your grandmother by proxy. I intended to-day to dress the convicts in prison garb, and you shall immediately be so clothed."

"I shall require seventeen suits," said the Jolly-cum-pop.

"Yes," said the jailer, "they shall be furnished."

"And seventeen rations a day," said the Jolly-cum-pop.

"Certainly," replied the jailer.

"This is luxury," roared the Jolly-cum-pop. "I shall spend my whole time in eating and putting on clean clothes."

Seventeen large prison suits were now brought to the Jolly-cum-pop. He put one on, and hung up the rest in his cell. These suits were half bright yellow and half bright green, with spots of bright red, as big as saucers.

The jailer now had doors cut from one cell to another. "If the Potentate comes here and wants to look at the prisoners," he said to the Jolly-cum-pop, "you must appear in cell number One, so that he can look through the hole in the door, and see you; then, as he walks along the corridor, you must walk through the cells, and whenever he looks into a cell, you must be there."

"He will think," merrily replied the Jolly-cum-pop,

"that all your prisoners are very fat, and that the little girls have grown up into big men."

"I will endeavor to explain that," said the jailer.

For several days the Jolly-cum-pop was highly amused at the idea of his being seventeen criminals, and he would sit first in one cell and then in another, trying to look like a ferocious pirate, a hard-hearted usurer, or a mean-spirited chicken thief, and laughing heartily at his failures. But, after a time, he began to tire of this, and to have a strong desire to see what sort of a tunnel the Prince's miners and rock-splitters were making under his house. "I had hoped," he said to himself, "that I should pine away in confinement, and so be able to get through the window-bars; but with nothing to do, and seventeen rations a day, I see no chance of that. But I must get out of this jail, and, as there seems no other way, I will revolt." Thereupon he shouted to the jailer through the hole in the door of his cell: "We have revolted! We have risen in a body, and have determined to resist your authority, and break jail!"

When the jailer heard this, he was greatly troubled. "Do not proceed to violence," he said; "let us parley."

"Very well," replied the Jolly-cum-pop, "but you must open the cell door. We cannot parley through a hole."

The jailer thereupon opened the cell door, and the Jolly-cum-pop, having wrapped sixteen suits of clothes around his left arm as a shield, and holding in his right hand the iron bar which had been cut from his window, stepped boldly into the corridor, and confronted the jailer and his myrmidons.

"It will be useless for you to resist," he said. "You are but four, and we are seventeen. If you had been wise you would have made us all cheating shop-keepers, chicken thieves, or usurers. Then you might have been able to control us; but when you see before you a desperate highwayman, a daring smuggler, a blood-thirsty pirate, a wily poacher, a powerful ruffian, a reckless burglar, a bold conspirator, and a murderer by proxy, you well may tremble!"

The jailer and his myrmidons looked at each other in dismay.

"We sigh for no blood," continued the Jolly-cum-pop, "and will readily agree to terms. We will give you your choice: Will you allow us to honorably surrender, and peacefully disperse to our homes, or shall we rush upon you in a body, and, after overpowering you by numbers, set fire to the jail, and escape through the crackling timbers of the burning pile?"

The jailer reflected for a minute. "It would be better, perhaps," he said, "that you should surrender and disperse to your homes."

The Jolly-cum-pop agreed to these terms, and the great gate being opened, he marched out in good order. "Now," said he to himself, "the thing for me to do is to get home as fast as I can, or that jailer may change his mind." But, being in a great hurry, he turned the wrong way, and walked rapidly into a country unknown to him. His walk was a very merry one. "By this time," he said to himself, "the Prince and his followers have returned to my house, and are tired of watching the rock-splitters and miners. How amused they will be when they see me come back in this gay suit of green and yellow, with red spots, and with sixteen similar suits upon my arm! How my own dogs will bark at me! And how my own servants will not know me! It is the funniest thing I ever knew of!" And his gay laugh echoed far and wide. But when he had gone several miles without seeing any signs of his habitation, his gayety abated. "It would have been much better," he said, as he sat down to rest under the shade of a tree, "if I had brought with me sixteen rations instead of these sixteen suits of clothes."

The Jolly-cum-pop soon set out again, but he walked a long distance without seeing any person or any house. Toward the close of the afternoon he stopped, and, looking back, he saw coming toward him a large party of foot travellers. In a few moments, he perceived that the person in advance was the jailer. At this the Jolly-cum-pop could not restrain his merriment. "How comically it has all turned out!" he exclaimed. "Here I've taken all this trouble, and tired myself out, and have nearly starved myself, and the jailer comes now, with a crowd of people, and takes me back. I might as well have staid where I was. Ha! ha!"

The jailer now left his party and came running toward the Jolly-cum-pop. "I pray you, sir," he said, bowing very low, "do not cast us off."

"Who are you all?" asked the Jolly-cum-pop,

looking with much surprise at the jailer's companions, who were now quite near.

"We are myself, my three myrmidons, and our wives and children. Our situations were such good ones that we married long ago, and our families lived in the upper stories of the prison. But when all the convicts had left we were afraid to remain, for, should the Potentate again visit the prison, he would be disappointed and enraged at finding no prisoners, and would, probably, punish us grievously. So we determined to follow you, and to ask you to let us go with you, wherever you are going. I wrote a report, which I fastened to the great gate, and in it I stated that sixteen of the convicts escaped by the aid of outside confederates, and that seventeen of them mutinied in a body and broke jail."

"That report," laughed the Jolly-cum-pop, "your Potentate will not readily understand."

"If I were there," said the jailer, "I could explain it to him; but, as it is, he must work it out for himself."

"Have you any thing to eat with you?" asked the Jolly-cum-pop.

"Oh, yes," said the jailer, "we brought provisions."

"Well, then, I gladly take you under my protection. Let us have supper. I have had nothing to eat since morning, and the weight of sixteen extra suits of clothes does not help to refresh one."

The Jolly-cum-pop and his companions slept that night under some trees, and started off early the next morning. "If I could only get myself turned in the proper direction," said he, " I believe we should soon reach my house.

The Prince, his courtiers, the boys and girls, the course-marker, and the map-maker worked industriously for several days at the foundation of their city. They dug the ground, they carried stones, they cut down trees. This work was very hard for all of them, for they were not used to it. After a few days' labor, the Prince said to the man with the red beard, who was reading his book : " I think we have now formed a nucleus. Any one can see that this is intended to be a city."

" No," said the man with the red beard, " nothing is truly a nucleus until something is gathered around it. Proceed with your work, while I continue my studies upon civil government."

Toward the close of that day the red-bearded man raised his eyes from his book and beheld the Jolly-cum-pop and his party approaching. " Hurrah ! " he cried, " we are already attracting settlers ! " And he went forth to meet them.

When the prince and the courtiers saw the Jolly-cum-pop in his bright and variegated dress, they did not know him ; but the boys and girls soon recognized his jovial face, and, tired as they were, they set up a hearty laugh, in which they were loudly joined by their merry friend. While the Jolly-cum-pop was listening to the adventures of the Prince and his companions, and telling what had happened to himself, the man with the red beard was talking to the jailer and his party, and urging them to gather around the nucleus which had been here formed, and help to build a city.

"Nothing will suit us better," exclaimed the jailer, "and the sooner we build a town wall so as to keep off the Potentate, if he should come this way, the better shall we be satisfied."

The next morning, the Prince said to the red-bearded man: "Others have gathered around us. We have formed a nucleus, and thus have done all that we promised to do. We shall now depart."

The man objected strongly to this, but the Prince paid no attention to his words. "What troubles me most," he said to the Jolly-cum-pop, "is the disgraceful condition of our clothes. They have been so torn and soiled during our unaccustomed work that they are not fit to be seen."

"As for that," said the Jolly-cum-pop, "I have sixteen suits with me, in which you can all dress, if you like. They are of unusual patterns, but they are new and clean."

"It is better," said the Prince, "for persons in my station to appear inordinately gay than to be seen in rags and dirt. We will accept your clothes."

Thereupon, the Prince and each of the others put on a prison dress of bright green and yellow, with large red spots. There were some garments left over, for each boy wore only a pair of trousers with the waistband tied around his neck, and holes cut for his arms; while the large jackets, with the sleeves tucked, made very good dresses for the girls. The Prince and his party, accompanied by the Jolly-cum-pop, now left the red-bearded man and his new settlers to continue the building of the city, and set off on their journey. The course-marker had not been informed the night before that they were to go away that morning, and consequently did not set his instrument by the stars.

" As we do not know in which way we should go," said the Prince, " one way will be as good as another, and if we can find a road let us take it; it will be easier walking."

In an hour or two they found a road and they took it. After journeying the greater part of the day, they reached the top of a low hill, over which the road ran, and saw before them a glittering sea and the spires and houses of a city.

" It is the city of Yan," said the course-marker.

" That is true," said the Prince; " and as we are so near, we may as well go there."

The astonishment of the people of Yan, when this party, dressed in bright green and yellow, with red spots, passed through their streets, was so great that the Jolly-cum-pop roared with laughter. This set the boys and girls and all the people laughing, and the sounds of merriment became so uproarious that when they reached the palace the King came ou to see what was the matter. What he thought when he saw his nephew in his fantastic guise, accompanied by a party apparently composed of sixteen other lunatics, cannot now be known; but, after hearing the Prince's story, he took him into an inner apartment, and thus addressed him : " My dear Hassak : The next time you pay me a visit, I beg for your sake and my own, that you will come in the ordinary way. You have sufficiently shown to the world that, when a Prince desires to travel, it is often necessary for him to go out of his way on account of obstacles."

"My dear uncle," replied Hassak, "your words shall not be forgotten."

After a pleasant visit of a few weeks, the Prince and his party (in new clothes) returned (by sea) to Itoby, whence the Jolly-cum-pop soon repaired to his home. There he found the miners and rock-splitters still at work at the tunnel, which had now penetrated half-way through the hill on which stood his house. "You may go home," he said, "for the Prince has changed his plans. I will put a door to this tunnel, and it will make an excellent cellar in which to keep my wine and provisions."

The day after the Prince's return his map-maker said to him: "Your Highness, according to your commands I made, each day, a map of your progress to the city of Yan. Here it is."

The Prince glanced at it and then he cast his eyes upon the floor. "Leave me," he said. "I would be alone."

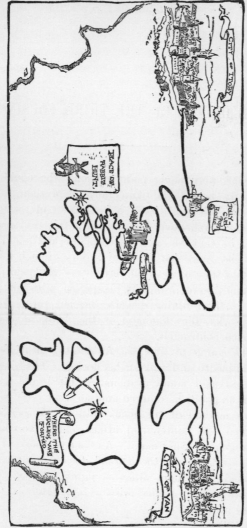

THE MAP OF THE PRINCE'S JOURNEY FROM ITOBY TO YAN.

THE BATTLE OF THE THIRD COUSINS.

THERE were never many persons who could correctly bound the Autocracy of Mutjado. The reason for this was that the boundary line was not stationary. Whenever the Autocrat felt the need of money, he sent his tax-gatherers far and wide, and people who up to that time had no idea of such a thing found that they lived in the territory of Mutjado. But when times were ordinarily prosperous with him, and people in the outlying districts needed protection or public works, the dominion of the Autocrat became very much contracted.

In the course of time, the Autocrat of Mutjado fell into bad health and sent for his doctor. That learned man prescribed some medicine for him; and as this did him no good, he ordered another kind. He continued this method of treatment until the Autocrat had swallowed the contents of fifteen phials and flasks, some large and some small. As none of these were of the slightest benefit, the learned doctor produced another kind of medicine which he highly extolled.

"Take a dose of this twice a day," said he, "and you will soon find ——"

138

"A new medicine?" interrupted the Autocrat, in disgust. "I will have none of it! These others were bad enough, and rather than start with a new physic, I prefer to die. Take away your bottles, little and big, and send me my secretary."

When that officer arrived, the Autocrat informed him that he had determined to write his will, and that he should set about it at once.

The Autocrat of Mutjado had no son, and his nearest male relatives were a third cousin on his father's side, and another third cousin on his mother's side. Of course these persons were in nowise related to each other; and as they lived in distant countries, he had never seen either of them. He had made up his mind to leave his throne and dominions to one of these persons, but he could not determine which of them should be his heir.

"One has as good a right as the other," he said to himself, "and I can't bother my brains settling the matter for them. Let them fight it out, and whoever conquers shall be Autocrat of Mutjado."

Having arranged the affair in this manner in his will, he signed it, and soon after died.

The Autocrat's third cousin on his father's side was a young man of about twenty-five, named Alberdin. He was a good horseman, and trained in the arts of warfare, and when he was informed of the terms of his distinguished relative's will, he declared himself perfectly willing to undertake the combat for the throne. He set out for Mutjado, where he arrived in a reasonable time.

The third cousin on the mother's side was a very different person. He was a boy of about twelve years of age ; and as his father and mother had died when he was very young, he had been for nearly all his life under the charge of an elderly and prudent man, who acted as his guardian and tutor. These two, also, soon arrived in Mutjado, — the boy, Phedo, being mounted on a little donkey, which was his almost constant companion. As soon as they reached the territory of the late Autocrat, old Salim, the tutor, left the boy at an inn, and went forward by himself to take a look at the other third cousin. When he saw Alberdin mounted on his fine horse, and looking so strong and valiant, his heart was much disturbed.

"I had hoped," he said to himself, " that the other one was a small boy, but such does not appear to be the case. There is but one way to have a fair fight between these two. They must not now be allowed to see each other. If they can be kept apart until my boy grows up, he will then be able, with the military education which I intend he shall have, to engage in combat with any man. They must not meet for at least thirteen years. Phedo will then be twenty-five, and able to do worthy combat. To be sure, I am somewhat old myself to undertake to superintend so long a delay, but I must do my best to keep well and strong, and to attain the greatest possible longevity."

Salim had always been in the habit of giving thirty-two chews to every mouthful of meat, and a proportionate number of chews to other articles of food ; and had, so far, been very healthy. But he now determined to increase the number of chews to thirty-six, for it would be highly necessary for him to live until it was time for the battle between the third cousins to take place.

Having made up his mind on these points, the old tutor introduced himself to Alberdin, and told him that he had come to arrange the terms of combat.

" In the first place," said Alberdin, " I should like to know what sort of a person my opponent is."

" He is not a cavalryman like you," answered Salim ; " he belongs to the heavy infantry."

At this, Alberdin looked grave. He knew very well that a stout and resolute man on foot had often the advantage of one who is mounted. He would have preferred meeting a horseman, and fighting on equal terms.

" Has he had much experience in war? " asked the young man.

" It is not long," answered the tutor, " since he was almost constantly in arms, winter and summer."

" He must be a practised warrior," thought Alberdin. " I must put myself in good fighting-trim before I meet him."

After some further conversation on the subject, the old man advised Alberdin to go into camp on a beautiful plain not far from the base of a low line of mountains.

" Your opponent," said he, " will intrench himself in the valley on the other side. With the mountains between you, neither of you need fear a surprise ; and when both are ready, a place of meeting can be appointed.

"Now, then," said Salim to himself when this had been settled; "if I can keep them apart for thirteen years, all may be well."

As soon as possible, Alberdin pitched a tent upon the appointed spot, and began to take daily warlike exercise in the plain, endeavoring in every way to put himself and his horse into proper condition for the combat.

On the other side of the mountain, old Salim intrenched himself and the boy, Phedo. He carefully studied several books on military engineering, and caused a fortified camp to be constructed on the most approved principles. It was surrounded by high ramparts, and outside of these was a moat filled with water. In the centre of the camp was a neat little house which was well provided with books, provisions, and every thing necessary for a prolonged stay. When the drawbridge was up, it would be impossible for Alberdin to get inside of the camp; and, moreover, the ramparts were so high that he could not look over them to see what sort of antagonist he was to have. Old Salim did not tell the boy why he brought him here to live. It would be better to wait until he was older before informing him of the battle which had been decreed. He told Phedo that it was necessary for him to have a military education, which could very well be obtained in a place like this; and he was also very careful to let him know that there was a terrible soldier in that part of the country who might at any time, if it were not for the intrenchments, pounce down upon him, and cut him to pieces. Every fine day, Phedo was allowed to take a ride on his donkey outside of the fortifications, but during this time, the old tutor kept a strict watch on the mountain; and if a horseman had made his appearance, little Phedo would have been whisked inside, and the drawbridge would have been up in a twinkling.

After about two weeks of this life Phedo found it dreadfully stupid to see no one but his old tutor, and never to go outside of these great ramparts except for donkey-rides, which were generally very short. He therefore determined, late one moonlight night, to go out and take a ramble by himself. He was not afraid of the dreadful soldier of whom the old man had told him, because at that time of night this personage would, of course, be in bed and asleep. Considering these things, he quietly dressed himself, took down a great key from over his sleeping tutor's head, opened the heavy gate, let down the drawbridge, mounted upon his donkey, and rode forth upon the moonlit plain.

That night-ride was a very delightful one, and for a long time the boy and the donkey rambled and ran; first going this way and then that, they gradually climbed the mountain; and, reaching the brow, they trotted about for a while, and then went down the other side. The boy had been so twisted and turned in his course that he did not notice that he was not descending toward his camp, and the donkey, whose instinct told it that it was not going the right way, was also told by its instinct that it did not wish to go the right way, and that the intrenchments offered it no tempta-

tions to return. When the morning dawned, Phedo
perceived that he was really lost, and he began to be
afraid that he might meet the terrible soldier. But,
after a time, he saw riding toward him a very pleasant-
looking young man on a handsome horse, and he
immediately took courage.

"Now," said he to himself, "I am no longer in
danger. If that horrible cut-throat should appear,
this good gentleman will protect me."

Alberdin had not seen any one for a long time, and
he was very glad to meet with so nice a little boy.
When Phedo told him that he was lost, he invited him
to come to his tent, near by, and have breakfast.
While they were eating their meal, Alberdin asked the
boy if in the course of his rambles he had met with a
heavy infantry soldier, probably armed to the teeth,
and very large and strong.

"Oh, I've heard of that dreadful man!" cried
Phedo, "and I am very glad that I did not meet him.
If he comes, I hope you'll protect me from him."

"I will do that," said Alberdin; "but I am afraid I
shall not be able to help you find your way home, for
in doing so I should throw myself off my guard, and
might be set upon unexpectedly by this fellow, with
whom I have a regular engagement to fight. There is
to be a time fixed for the combat, for which I feel myself nearly ready, but I have no doubt that my enemy
will be very glad to take me at a disadvantage if I give
him a chance."

Phedo looked about him with an air of content. The
tent was large and well furnished; there seemed to be

plenty of good things to eat; the handsome horseman was certainly a very good-humored and agreeable gentleman; and, moreover, the tent was not shut in by high and gloomy ramparts.

"I do not think you need trouble yourself," said he to his host, "to help me to find my way home. I live with my tutor, and I am sure that when he knows I am gone he will begin to search for me, and after awhile he will find me. Until then, I can be very comfortable here."

For several days the two third cousins of the Autocrat lived together in the tent, and enjoyed each other's society very much. Then Alberdin began to grow a little impatient.

"If I am to fight this heavy infantry man," he said; "I should like to do it at once. I am now quite ready, and I think he ought to be. I expected to hear from him before this time, and I shall start out and see if I can get any news of his intentions. I don't care about going over the mountain without giving him notice, but the capital city of Mutjado is only a day's ride to the west, and there I can cause inquiries to be made when he would like to meet me, and where."

"I will go with you," said Phedo, greatly delighted at the idea of visiting the city.

"Yes, I will take you," said Alberdin. "Your tutor don't seem inclined to come for you, and, of course, I can't leave you here."

The next day, Alberdin on his horse, and Phedo on his donkey, set out for the city, where they arrived late in the afternoon. After finding a comfortable lodging, Alberdin sent messengers to the other side of the mountain, where his opponent was supposed to be encamped, and gave them power to arrange with him for a meeting. He particularly urged them to try to see the old man who had come to him at first, and who had seemed to be a very fair-minded and sensible person. In two days, however, the messengers returned, stating that they had found what they supposed to be the intrenched camp of the heavy infantry man they had been sent in search of, but that it was entirely deserted, and nobody could be seen anywhere near it.

" It is very likely," said Alberdin, " that he has watched my manoeuvres and exercises from the top of the mountain, and has concluded to run away. I shall give him a reasonable time to show himself, and then, if he does not come forward, I will consider him beaten, and claim the Autocracy."

" That is a good idea," said Phedo, " but I think, if you can, you ought to find him and kill him, or drive him out of the country. That's what I should do, if I were you."

" Of course I shall do that, if I can," said Alberdin ; " but I could not be expected to wait for him forever."

When his intention had been proclaimed, Alberdin was informed of something which he did not know before, and that was that the late Autocrat had left an only daughter, a Princess about twenty years old. But although she was his daughter, she could not inherit his crown, for the laws of the country forbade that any woman should become Autocrat. A happy idea now struck Alberdin.

" I will marry the Princess," he said, " and then every one will think that it is the most suitable thing for me to become Autocrat."

So Alberdin sent to the Princess to ask permission to speak with her, and was granted an audience. With much courtesy and politeness he made known his plans to the lady, and hoped that she would consider it advisable to marry him.

" I am sorry to interfere with any of your arrangements," said the Princess, " but as soon as I heard the terms of my father's will, I made up my mind to marry the victor in the contest. As I cannot inherit the throne myself, the next best thing is to be the wife of the man who does. Go forth, then, and find your antagonist, and when you have conquered him, I will marry you."

" And if he conquers me, you will marry him?" said Alberdin.

" Yes, sir," answered the Princess, with a smile, and dismissed him.

It was plain enough that there was nothing for Alberdin to do but to go and look for the heavy infantry man. Phedo was very anxious to accompany him, and the two, mounted as before, set out from the city on their quest.

When old Salim, the tutor of Phedo, awoke in the morning and found the boy gone, he immediately imagined that the youngster had run away to his old home ; so he set forth with all possible speed, hoping to overtake him. But when he reached the distant town where Phedo had lived, he found that the boy had not been there; and after taking some needful rest, he retraced his steps, crossed the mountains, and made his way toward the capital city, hoping to find news of him there. It was necessary for him to be very careful in his inquiries, for he wished no one to find out that the little boy he was looking for was the third cousin of the late Autocrat on the mother's side. He therefore disguised himself as a migratory medical man, and determined to use all possible caution. When he reached the camp of the young horseman, Alberdin, and found that personage gone, his suspicions became excited.

"If these two have run off together," he said to himself, "my task is indeed difficult. If the man discovers it is the boy he has to fight, my poor Phedo will be cut to pieces in a twinkling. I do not believe there has been any trouble yet, for the boy does not know that he is to be one of the combatants, and the man would not be likely to suspect it. Come what may, the fight must not take place for thirteen years. And in order that I may still better preserve my health and strength to avert the calamity during that period, I will increase my number of chews to forty-two to each mouthful of meat."

When old Salm reached the city, he soon found that Alberdin and the boy had been there, and that they had gone away together.

"Nothing has happened so far," said the old man, with a sigh of relief; "and things may turn out all right yet. I'll follow them, but I must first find out what that cavalryman had to say to the Princess." For he had been told of the interview at the palace.

It was not long before the migratory medical man was brought to the Princess. There was nothing the matter with her, but she liked to meet with persons of skill and learning to hear what they had to say.

" Have you any specialty?" she asked of the old man.

" Yes," said he, " I am a germ-doctor."

" What is that?" asked the Princess.

" All diseases," replied the old man, " come from germs ; generally very little ones. My business is to discover these, and find out all about them."

" Then I suppose," said the Princess, " you know how to cure the diseases?"

" You must not expect too much," answered the old man. " It ought to be a great satisfaction to us to know what sort of germ is at the bottom of our woes."

" I am very well, myself," said the Princess, " and, so far as I know, none of my household are troubled by germs. But there is something the matter with my mind which I wish you could relieve." She then told the old man how she had determined to marry the victor in the contest for her father's throne, and how she had seen one for the claimants whom she considered to be a very agreeable and deserving young man ; while the other, she had heard, was a great, strong foot soldier, who was probably very disagreeable, and even horrid. If this one should prove the conqueror, she did not know what she should do. " You see, I am in a great deal of trouble," said she. " Can you do any thing to help me?"

The pretending migratory medical man looked at her attentively for a few moments, and then he said:

" The reason why you intend to marry the victor in the coming contest, is that you wish to remain here in your father's palace, and to continue to enjoy the comforts and advantages to which you have been accustomed."

" Yes," said the Princess ; " that is it."

" Well, having discovered the germ of your disorder," said the old man, " the great point is gained. I will see what I can do."

And with a respectful bow he left her presence.

" Well," said old Salim to himself, as he went away, " she can never marry my boy, for that is certainly out of the question ; but now that I have found out her motive, I think I can arrange matters satisfactorily, so far as she is concerned. But to settle the affair between that young man and Phedo is immensely more difficult. The first thing is to find them."

Having learned the way they had gone, the old tutor travelled diligently, and in two days came up with Alberdin and Phedo. When he first caught sight of them, he was very much surprised to see that they were resting upon the ground quite a long distance apart, with a little stream between them. Noticing that Alberdin's back was toward him, he threw off his disguise and hastened to Phedo. The boy received him with the greatest delight, and, after many embraces, they sat down to talk. Phedo told the old man all that had happened, and finished by relating that, as they had that day stopped by this stream to rest, Alberdin had taken it into his head to inquire into the parentage of his young companion; and after many questions about his family, it had been made clear to both of them that they were the two third cousins who were to fight for the Autocracy of Mutjado.

"He is very angry," said the boy, "at the tricks that have been played upon him, and went off and left me. Is it true that I am to fight him? I don't want to do it, for I like him very much."

"It will be a long time before you are old enough to fight," said Salim; "so we need not consider that. You stay here, and I'll go over and talk to him."

Salim then crossed the stream, and approached Alberdin. When the young man saw him, and recognized him as the person who had arranged the two encampments, he turned upon him with fury.

"Wretched old man, who came to me as the emissary of my antagonist, you are but the tutor of that boy! If I had known the truth at first, I would have met him instantly; would have conquered him without hurting a hair on his head; and carrying him bound to the capital city, would have claimed the Autocracy, and would now have been sitting upon the throne. Instead of that, look at the delay and annoyance to which I have been subjected. I have also taken such a fancy to the boy that rather than hurt him or injure his prospects, I would willingly resign my pretensions to the throne, and go back contentedly to my own city.

But this cannot now be done. I have fallen in love with the daughter of the late Autocrat, and she will marry none but the victorious claimant. Behold to what a condition you have brought me!"

The old man regarded him with attention.

"I wish very much," said he, "to defer the settlement of this matter for thirteen years. Are you willing to wait so long?"

"No, I am not," said Alberdin.

"Very well, then," said the old man, "each third cousin must retire to his camp, and as soon as matters can be arranged the battle must take place."

"There is nothing else to be done," said Alberdin in a troubled voice; "but I shall take care that the boy receives no injury if it can possibly be avoided."

The three now retraced their steps, and in a few days were settled down, Alberdin in his tent in the plain, and Salim and Phedo in their intrenchments on the other side of the low mountain. The old man now gave himself up to deep thought. He had discovered the germ of Alberdin's trouble; and in a few days he had arranged his plans, and went over to see the young man.

"It has been determined," said he, "that a syndicate is to be formed to attend to this business for Phedo."

"A syndicate!" cried Alberdin. "What is that?"

"A syndic," answered Salim, "is a person who attends to business for others; and a syndicate is a body of men who are able to conduct certain affairs better than any individual can do it. In a week from to-day, Phedo's syndicate will meet you in the large plain outside of the capital city. There the contest will take place. Shall you be ready?"

"I don't exactly understand it," said Alberdin, "but I shall be there."

General notice was given of the coming battle of the contestants for the throne, and thousands of the inhabitants of the Autocracy assembled on the plain on the appointed day. The Princess with her ladies was there ; and as everybody was interested, everybody was anxious to see what would happen.

Alberdin rode into the open space in the centre of the plain, and demanded that his antagonist should appear. Thereupon old Salim came forward, leading Phedo by the hand.

"This is the opposing heir," he said ; "but as every one can see that he is too young to fight a battle, a syndicate has been appointed to attend to the matter for him ; and there is nothing in the will of the late Autocrat which forbids this arrangement. The syndicate will now appear."

At this command there came into the arena a horseman heavily armed, a tall foot soldier completely equipped for action, an artilleryman with a small cannon on wheels, a sailor with a boarding-pike and a drawn cutlass, and a soldier with a revolving gun which discharged one hundred and twenty balls a minute.

"All being ready," exclaimed Salim, "the combat for the Autocracy will begin!"

Alberdin took a good long look at the syndicate ranged before him. Then he dismounted from his horse, drew his sword, and stuck it, point downward, into the sand.

" I surrender ! " he said.

" So do I ! " cried the Princess, running toward him, and throwing herself into his arms.

The eyes of Alberdin sparkled with joy.

" Let the Autocracy go ! " he cried. " Now that I have my Princess, the throne and the crown are nothing to me."

" So long as I have you," returned the Princess, " I am content to resign all the comforts and advantages to which I have been accustomed."

Phedo, who had been earnestly talking with his tutor, now looked up.

" You shall not resign any thing ! " he cried. " We are all of the same blood, and we will join together and form a royal family, and we will all live at the palace. Alberdin and my tutor shall manage the government for me until I am grown up ; and if I have to go to school for a few years, I suppose I must. And that is all there is about it ! "

The syndicate was now ordered to retire and disband ; the heralds proclaimed Phedo the conquering heir, and the people cheered and shouted with delight. All the virtues of the late Autocrat had come to him from his mother, and the citizens of Mutjado much preferred to have a new ruler from the mother's family.

" I hope you bear no grudge against me," said Salim to Alberdin ; " but if you had been willing to wait for thirteen years, you and Phedo might have fought on equal terms. As it is now, it would have been as hard for him to conquer you, as for you to conquer the syndicate. The odds would have been quite as great."

"Don't mention it," said Alberdin. "I prefer things as they are. I should have hated to drive the boy away, and deprive him of a position which the people wish him to have. Now we are all satisfied."

Phedo soon began to show signs that he would probably make a very good Autocrat. He declared that if he was to be assisted by ministers and cabinet officers when he came to the throne, he would like them to be persons who had been educated for their positions, just as he was to be educated for his own. Consequently he chose for the head of his cabinet a bright and sensible boy, and had him educated as a Minister of State. For Minister of Finance, he chose another boy with a very honest countenance, and for the other members of his cabinet, suitable youths were selected. He also said, that he thought there ought to be another officer, one who would be a sort of Minister of General Comfort, who would keep an eye on the health and happiness of the subjects, and would also see that every thing went all right in the palace, not only in regard to meals, but lots of other things. For this office he chose a bright young girl, and had her educated for the position of Queen.

THE BANISHED KING.

THERE was once a kingdom in which every thing seemed to go wrong. Everybody knew this, and everybody talked about it, especially the King. The bad state of affairs troubled him more than it did any one else, but he could think of no way to make them better.

"I cannot bear to see things going on so badly," he said to the Queen and his chief councillors. "I wish I knew how other kingdoms were governed."

One of his councillors offered to go to some other countries, and see how they were governed, and come back and tell him all about it, but this did not suit his majesty.

"You would simply return," he said, "and give me your ideas about things. I want my own ideas."

The Queen then suggested that he should take a vacation, and visit other kingdoms, and see for himself how things were managed in them.

This did not suit the king. "A vacation would not answer," he said. "I should not be gone a week before something would happen here which would make it necessary for me to come back."

156

The Queen then suggested that he be banished for a certain time, say a year. In that case he could not come back, and would be at full liberty to visit foreign kingdoms, and find out how they were governed.

This plan pleased the King. "If it were made impossible for me to come back," he said, "of course I could not do it. The scheme is a good one. Let me be banished." And he gave orders that his council should pass a law banishing him for one year.

Preparations were immediately begun to carry out this plan, and in day or two the King bade farewell to the Queen, and left his kingdom, a banished man. He went away on foot, entirely unattended. But, as he did not wish to cut off all communication between himself and his kingdom, he made an arrangement which he thought a very good one. At easy shouting distance behind him walked one of the officers of the court, and at shouting distance behind him walked another, and so on at distances of about a hundred yards from each other. In this way there would always be a line of men extending from the King to his palace. Whenever the King had walked a hundred yards the line moved on after him, and another officer was put in the gap between the last man and the palace door. Thus, as the King walked on, his line of followers lengthened, and was never broken. Whenever he had any message to send to the Queen, or any other person in the palace, he shouted it to the officer next him, who shouted it to the one next to him, and it was so passed on until it reached the palace. If he needed food, clothes, or any other necessary thing, the order for it was shouted along the line, and the article was passed to him from man to man, each one carrying it forward to his neighbor, and then retiring to his proper place.

In this way the King walked on day by day until he had passed entirely out of his own kingdom. At night he stopped at some convenient house on the road, and if any of his followers did not find himself near a house or cottage when the King shouted back the order to halt, he laid himself down to sleep wherever he might be. By this time the increasing line of followers had used up all the officers of the court, and it became necessary to draw upon some of the under government officers in order to keep the line perfect.

The King had not gone very far outside the limits of his dominions when he met a Sphinx. He had often heard of these creatures, although he had never seen one before. But when he saw the winged body of a lion with a woman's head, he knew instantly what it was. He knew, also, that the chief business of a Sphinx was that of asking people questions, and then getting them into trouble if the right answers were not given. He therefore determined that he would not be caught by any such tricks as these, and that he would be on his guard if the Sphinx spoke to him. The creature was lying down when the King first saw it, but when he approached nearer it rose to its feet. There was nothing savage about its look, and the King was not at all afraid.

"Where are you going?" said the Sphinx to him, in a pleasant voice.

" Give it up," replied the King.

" What do you mean by that ? " said the other, with an air of surprise.

" I give that up, too," said the King.

The Sphinx then looked at him quite astonished.

" I don't mind telling you," said the King, " of my own free will, and not in answer to any questions, that I do not know where I am going. I am a King, as you may have noticed, and I have been banished from my kingdom for a year. I am now going to look into the government of other countries in order that I may find out what it is that is wrong in my own kingdom. Every thing goes badly, and there is something very faulty at the bottom of it all. What this is I want to discover."

" I am much interested in puzzles and matters of that kind," said the Sphinx, " and if you like I will go with you and help to find out what is wrong in your kingdom."

" All right," said the king. " I shall be glad of your company."

" What is the meaning of this long line of people following you at regular distances? " asked the Sphinx.

" Give it up," said the King.

The Sphinx laughed.

" I don't mind telling you," said the King, " of my own free will, and not in answer to any question, that these men form a line of communication between me and my kingdom, where matters, I fear, must be going on worse than ever, in my absence."

The two now travelled on together until they came to a high hill, from which they could see, not very far away, a large city.

"That city," said the Sphinx, "is the capital of an extensive country. It is governed by a king of mingled sentiments. Suppose we go there. I think you will find a government that is rather peculiar."

The King consented, and they walked down the hill toward the city.

"How did the King get his sentiments mingled?" asked the King.

"I really don't know how it began," said the Sphinx, "but the King, when a young man, had so many sentiments of different kinds, and he mingled them up so much, that no one could ever tell exactly what he thought on any particular subject. Of course, his people gradually got into the same frame of mind, and you never can know in this kingdom exactly what people think or what they are going to do. You will find all sorts of people here: giants, dwarfs, fairies, gnomes, and personages of that kind, who have been drawn here by the mingled sentiments of the people. I, myself, came into these parts because the people every now and then take a great fancy to puzzles and riddles."

On entering the city, the King was cordially welcomed by his brother sovereign, to whom he told his story; and he was lodged in a room in the palace. Such of his followers as came within the limits of the city were entertained by the persons near to whose houses they found themselves when the line halted.

Every day the Sphinx went with him to see the sights of this strange city. They took long walks through the streets, and sometimes into the surrounding country — always going one way and returning another, the Sphinx being very careful never to bring the King back by the same road or street by which they went. In this way the King's line of followers, which, of course, lengthened out every time he took a walk, came to be arranged in long loops through many parts of the city and suburbs.

Many of the things the King saw showed plainly the mingled sentiments of the people. For instance, he would one day visit a great smith's shop, where heavy masses of iron were being forged, the whole place resounding with tremendous blows from heavy hammers, and the clank and din of iron on the anvils; while the next day he would find the place transformed into a studio, where the former blacksmith was painting dainty little pictures on the delicate surface of egg-shells. The king of the country, in his treatment of his visitor, showed his peculiar nature very plainly. Sometimes he would receive him with enthusiastic delight, while at others he would upbraid him with having left his dominions to go wandering around the earth in this senseless way. One day his host invited him to attend a royal dinner, but, when he went to the grand dining-hall, pleased with anticipations of a splendid feast, he found that the sentiments of his majesty had become mingled, and that he had determined, instead of having a dinner, to conduct the funeral services of one of his servants who had died the day before. All the guests were obliged by politeness to remain during the ceremonies, which our King, not having been acquainted with the deceased servant, had not found at all interesting.

"Now," said the King to the Sphinx, "I am in favor of moving on. I am tired of this place, where every sentiment is so mingled with others that you can never tell what anybody really thinks or feels. I don't believe any one in this country was ever truly glad or sorry. They mix one sentiment so quickly with another that they never can discover the actual ingredients of any of their impulses."

"When this King first began to mingle his sentiments," said the Sphinx, "it was because he always desired to think and feel exactly right. He did not wish his feelings to run too much one way or the other."

"And so he is never either right or wrong," said the King. "I don't like that, at all. I want to be one thing or the other."

"I have wasted a good deal of time at this place," remarked the King, as they walked on, "and I have seen and heard nothing which I wish to teach my people. But I must find out some way to prevent every thing going wrong in my kingdom. I have tried plan after plan, and sometimes two or three together, and have kept this up year after year, and yet nothing seems to do my kingdom any good."

"Have you heard how things are going on there now?" asked the Sphinx.

"Give it up," said the King. "But I don't mind

saying of my own accord, and not as answer to any question, that I have sent a good many communications to my Queen, but have never received any from her. So I do not know how things are going on in my kingdom.''

They then travelled on, the long line of followers coming after, keeping their relative positions a hundred yards apart, and passing over all the ground the King had traversed in his circuitous walks about the city. Thus the line crept along like an enormous snake in straight lines, loops, and coils; and every time the King walked a hundred yards a fresh man from his capital city was obliged to take his place at the tail of the procession.

'' By the way,'' said the Sphinx, after they had walked an hour or more, '' if you want to see a kingdom where there really is something to learn, you ought to go to the country of the Gaumers, which we are now approaching.''

'' All right,'' said the King. '' Let us go there.''

In the course of the afternoon they reached the edge of a high bluff. '' On the level ground, beneath this precipice,'' said the Sphinx, '' is the country of the dwarfs called Gaumers. You can sit on the edge of the bluff and look down upon it.''

The King and the Sphinx then sat down, and looked out from the edge over the country of the little people. The officer of the court who had formed the head of the line wished very much to see what they were looking at, but, when the line halted, he was not near enough.

"You will notice," said the Sphinx, "that the little houses and huts are gathered together in clusters. Each one of these clusters is under a separate king.

"Why don't they all live under one ruler?" asked the King. "That is the proper way."

"They do not think so," said the Sphinx. "In each of these clusters live the Gaumers who are best suited to each other; and, if any Gaumer finds he cannot get along in one cluster, he goes to another. The kings are chosen from among the very best of them, and each one is always very anxious to please his subjects. He knows that every thing that he, and his queen, and his children eat, or drink, or wear, or have must be given to him by his subjects, and if it were not for them he could not be their ruler. And so he does every thing that he can to make them happy and contented, for he knows if he does not please them and govern them well, they will gradually drop off from him and go to other clusters, and he will be left without any people or any kingdom."

"That is a very queer way of ruling," said the King. "I think the people ought to try to please their sovereign."

"He is only one, and they are a great many," said the Sphinx. "Consequently they are much more important. No subject is ever allowed to look down upon a king, simply because he helps to feed and clothe him, and send his children to school. If any one does a thing of this kind, he is banished until he learns better."

"All that may be very well for Gaumers," said the

King, "but I can learn nothing from a government like that, where every thing seems to be working in an opposite direction from what everybody knows is right and proper. A king anxious to deserve the good opinion of his subjects! What nonsense! It ought to be just the other way. The ideas of this people are as dwarfish as their bodies."

The King now arose and took up the line of march, turning away from the country of the Gaumers. But he had not gone more than two or three hundred yards before he received a message from the Queen. It came to him very rapidly, every man in the line seeming anxious to shout it to the man ahead of him as quickly as possible. The messsge was to the effect that he must either stop where he was or come home: his constantly lengthening line of communication had used up all the chief officers of the government, all the clerks in the departments, and all the officials of every grade, excepting the few who were actually needed to carry on the government, and if any more men went into the line it would be necessary to call upon the laborers and other persons who could not be spared.

"I think," said the Sphinx, "that you have made your line long enough."

"And I think," said the King. "that you made it a great deal longer than it need to have been, by taking me about in such winding ways."

"It may be so," said the Sphinx, with its mystic smile.

"Well, I am not going to stop here," said the King, "and so I might as well go back as soon as I can."

And he shouted to the head man of the line to pass on the order that his edict of banishment be revoked.

In a very short time the news came that the edict was revoked. The King then commanded that the procession return home, tail-end foremost. The march was at once begun, each man, as he reached the city, going immediately to his home and family.

The King and the greater part of the line had a long and weary journey, as they followed each other through the country and over the devious ways in which the Sphinx had led them in the City of Mingled Sentiments. The King was obliged to pursue all these complicated turnings, or be separated from his officers, and so break up his communication with his palace. The Sphinx accompanied him.

When at last, he reached his palace, his line of former followers having apparently melted entirely away, he hurried up-stairs to the Queen, leaving the Sphinx in the court-yard.

The King found, when he had time to look into the affairs of his dominions, that every thing was in the most admirable condition. The Queen had retained a few of the best officials to carry on the government, and had ordered the rest to fall, one by one, into the line of communication. The King set himself to work to think about the matter. It was not long before he came to the conclusion that the main thing which had been wrong in his kingdom was himself. He was so greatly impressed with this idea that he went down to the court-yard to speak to the Sphinx about it.

" I dare say you are right," said the Sphinx, " and

I don't wonder that what you learned when you were away, and what you have seen since you came back, have made you feel certain that you were the cause of every thing going wrong in this kingdom. And now, what do you intend to do about your government?''

" Give it up," promptly replied the King.

" That is exactly what I should advise," said the Sphinx.

The King did give up his kingdom. He was convinced that being a King was exactly the thing he was not suited for, and that he would get on much better in some other business or profession. He determined to be a traveller and explorer, and to go abroad into other countries to find out things that might be useful to his own nation. His Queen had shown that she could govern the country most excellently, and it was not at all necessary for him to stay at home. She had ordered all the men who had made up his line to follow the King's example and to go into some good business; in order that not being bothered with so many officers, she would be able to get along quite easily.

The King was very successful in his new pursuit, and although he did not this time have a line of followers connecting him with the palace, he frequently sent home messages which were of use and value to his nation.

" I may as well retire," said the Sphinx to itself. " As the King has found his vocation and every thing is going all right it is not necessary I should remain where I may be looked upon as a questionable personage."

THE PHILOPENA.

THERE were once a Prince and a Princess who, when quite young, ate a philopena together. They agreed that the one who, at any hour after sunrise the next day, should accept any thing from the other —the giver at the same time saying "Philopena!"— should be the loser, and that the loser should marry the other.

They did not meet as soon as they had expected the next day; and at the time our story begins, many years had elapsed since they had seen each other, and the Prince and the Princess were nearly grown up. They often thought of the philopena they had eaten together, and wondered if they should know each other when they met. He remembered her as a pretty little girl dressed in green silk and playing with a snow-white cat; while she remembered him as a handsome boy, wearing a little sword, the handle of which was covered with jewels. But they knew that each must have changed a great deal in all this time.

Neither of these young people had any parents; the Prince lived with guardians and the Princess with uncles.

The guardians of the Prince were very enterprising and energetic men, and were allowed to govern the country until the Prince came of age. The capital city was a very fine city when the old king died; but the guardians thought it might be much finer, so they set to work with all their might and main to improve it. They tore down old houses and made a great many new streets; they built grand and splendid bridges over the river on which the city stood; they constructed aqueducts to bring water from streams many miles away; and they were at work all the time upon some extensive building enterprise.

The Prince did not take much interest in the works which were going on under direction of his guardians; and when he rode out, he preferred to go into the country or to ride through some of the quaint old streets, where nothing had been changed for hundreds of years.

The uncles of the Princess were very different people from the guardians of the Prince. There were three of them, and they were very quiet and cosey old men, who disliked any kind of bustle or disturbance, and wished that every thing might remain as they had always known it. It even worried them a little to find that the Princess was growing up. They would have much preferred that she should remain exactly as she was when they first took charge of her. Then they never would have been obliged to trouble their minds about any changes in the manner of taking care of her. But they did not worry their minds very much, after all. They wished to make her guardianship as little laborious or exhausting as possible, and so, divided the work; one of them took charge of her education, another of her food and lodging, and the third of her dress. The first sent for teachers, and told them to teach her; the second had handsome apartments prepared for her use, and gave orders that she should have every thing she needed to eat and drink; while the third commanded that she should have a complete outfit of new clothes four times a year. Thus every thing went on very quietly and smoothly; and the three uncles were not obliged to exhaust themselves by hard work. There were never any new houses built in that city, and if any thing had to be repaired, it was done with as little noise and dirt as possible. The city and the whole kingdon were quiet and serene, and the three uncles dozed away most of the day in three great comfortable thrones.

Everybody seemed satisfied with this state of things except the Princess. She often thought to herself that nothing would be more delightful than a little noise and motion, and she wondered if the whole world were as quiet as the city in which she lived. At last, she became unable to bear the dreadful stillness of the place any longer; but she could think of nothing to do but to go and try to find the Prince with whom she had eaten a philopena. If she should win, he must marry her; and then, perhaps, they could settle down in some place where things would be bright and lively. So, early one morning, she put on her white dress, and mounting her prancing black horse, she rode away from the city. Only one person saw her go, for nearly all the people were asleep.

About this time, the Prince made up his mind that he could no longer stand the din and confusion, the everlasting up-setting and setting-up in his native city. He would go away, and see if he could find the Princess with whom he had eaten a philopena. If he should win, she would be obliged to marry him; and then, perhaps, they could settle down in some place where it was quiet and peaceful. So, on the same morning in which the Princess rode away, he put on a handsome suit of black clothes, and mounting a gentle white horse, he rode out of the city. Only one person saw him go; for, even at that early hour, the people were so busy that little attention was paid to his movements.

About half way between these two cities, in a tall tower which stood upon a hill, there lived an Inquisitive Dwarf, whose whole object in life was to find out what people were doing and why they did it. From the top of this tower he generally managed to see all that was going on in the surrounding country; and in each of the two cities that have been mentioned he had an agent, whose duty it was to send him word, by means of carrier pigeons, whenever a new thing happened. Before breakfast, on the morning when the Prince and Princess rode away, a pigeon from the city of the Prince came flying to the tower of the Inquisitive Dwarf.

"Some new building started, I suppose," said the Dwarf, as he took the little roll of paper from under the pigeon's wing. "But no; it is very different! 'The Prince has ridden away from the city alone, and is travelling to the north.'"

But before he could begin to puzzle his brains about the meaning of this departure, another pigeon came flying in from the city of the Princess.

" Well ! " cried the Dwarf, " this is amazing ! It is a long time since I have had a message from that city, and my agent has been drawing his salary without doing any work. What possibly can have happened there ? "

When he read that the Princess had ridden alone from the city that morning, and was travelling to the south, he was truly amazed.

" What on earth can it mean ? " he exclaimed. " If the city of the Prince were to the south of that of the Princess, then I might understand it ; for they would be going to see each other, and that would be natural enough. But as his city is to the north of her city, they are travelling in opposite directions. And what is the meaning of this ? I most certainly must find out."

The Inquisitive Dwarf had three servants whom he employed to attend to his most important business. These were a Gryphoness, a Water Sprite, and an Absolute Fool. This last one was very valuable ; for there were some things he would do which no one else would think of attempting. The Dwarf called to him the Gryphoness, the oldest and most discreet of the three, and told her of the departure of the Princess.

" Hasten southward," he said, " as fast as you can, and follow her, and do not return to me until you have found out why she left her city, where she is going, and what she expects to do when she gets there.

Your appearance may frighten her; and, therefore, you must take with you the Absolute Fool, to whom she will probably be willing to talk; but you must see that every thing is managed properly.''

Having despatched these two, the Inquisitive Dwarf then called the Water Sprite, who was singing to herself at the edge of a fountain, and telling her of the departure of the Prince, ordered her to follow him, and not to return until she had found out why he left his city, where he was going, and what he intended to do when he got there.

''The road to the north,'' he said, ''lies along the river bank; therefore, you can easily keep him company.''

The Water Sprite bowed, and dancing over the dewy grass to the river, threw herself into it. Sometimes she swam beneath the clear water; sometimes she rose partly in the air, where she seemed like a little cloud of sparkling mist borne onward by the wind; and sometimes she floated upon the surface, her pale blue robes undulating with the gentle waves, while her white hands and feet shone in the sun like tiny crests of foam. Thus, singing to herself, she went joyously and rapidly on, aided by a full, strong wind from the south. She did not forget to glance every now and then upon the road which ran along the river bank; and, in the course of the morning, she perceived the Prince. He was sitting in the shade of a tree near the water's edge, while his white horse was grazing near by.

The Water Sprite came very gently out of the river,

and seating herself upon the edge of the grassy bank, she spoke to him. The Prince looked up in astonishment, but there was nothing in her appearance to frighten him.

" I came," said the Water Sprite, at the command of my master, to ask you why you left your city, where you are going, and what you intend to do when you get there."

The Prince then told her why he had left his city, and what he intended to do when he had found the Princess.

" But where I am going," he said, " I do not know, myself. I must travel and travel until I succeed in the object of my search."

The Water Sprite reflected for a moment, and then she said :

" If I were you, I would not travel to the north. It is cold and dreary there, and your Princess would not dwell in such a region. A little above us, on the other side of this river, there is a stream which runs sometimes to the east and sometimes to the south, and which leads to the Land of the Lovely Lakes. This is the most beautiful country in the world, and you will be much more likely to find your Princess there than among the desolate mountains of the north."

" I dare say you are right," said the Prince ; "and I will go there, if you will show me the way."

" The road runs along the bank of the river," said the Water Sprite ; " and we shall soon reach the Land of the Lovely Lakes."

The Prince then mounted his horse, forded the

river, and was soon riding along the bank of the stream, while the Water Sprite gayly floated upon its dancing ripples.

When the Gryphoness started southward, in pursuit of the Princess, she kept out of sight among the bushes by the roadside; but sped swiftly along. The Absolute Fool, however, mounted upon a fine horse, rode boldly along upon the open road. He was a good-looking youth, with rosy cheeks, bright eyes, and a handsome figure. As he cantered gayly along, he felt himself capable of every noble action which the human mind has ever conceived. The Gryphoness kept near him, and in the course of the morning they overtook the Princess, who was allowing her horse to walk in the shade by the roadside. The Absolute Fool dashed up to her, and, taking off his hat, asked her why she had left her city, where she was going, and what she intended to do when she got there.

The Princess looked at him in surprise. "I left my city because I wanted to," she said. "I am going about my business, and when I get to the proper place, I shall attend to it."

"Oh," said the Absolute Fool, " you refuse me your confidence, do you? But allow me to remark that I have a Gryphoness with me who is very frightful to look at, and whom it was my intention to keep in the bushes; but if you will not give fair answers to my questions, she must come out and talk to you, and that is all there is about it."

"If there is a Gryphoness in the bushes," said the

Princess, "let her come out. No matter how frightful she is, I would rather she should come where I can see her, than to have her hiding near me."

The Gryphoness, who had heard these words, now came out into the road. The horse of the Princess reared in affright, but his young rider patted him on the neck, and quieted his fears.

"What do you and this young man want?" said the Princess to the Gryphoness, "and why do you question me?"

"It is not of our own will that we do it," said the Gryphoness, very respectfully; "but our master, the Inquisitive Dwarf, has sent us to obtain information about the points on which the young man questioned you; and until we have found out these things, it is impossible for us to return."

"I am opposed to answering impertinent questions," replied the Princess; "but in order to rid myself of you, I will tell you the reason of my journey." And she then stated briefly the facts of the case.

"Ah, me!" said the Gryphoness. "I am very sorry; but you cannot tell us where you are going, and we cannot return until we know that. But you need not desire to be rid of us, for it may be that we can assist you in the object of your journey. This young man is sometimes very useful, and I shall be glad to do any thing that I can to help you. If you should think that I would injure you, or willingly annoy you by my presence, it would grieve me to the heart." And as she spoke, a tear bedimmed her eye.

The Princess was touched by the emotion of the Gryphoness.

"You may accompany me," she said, "and I will trust you both. You must know this country better than I do. Have you any advice to give me in regard to my journey?"

"One thing I would strongly advise," said the Gryphoness, "and that is, that you do not travel any farther until we know in what direction it will be best to go. There is an inn close by, kept by a worthy woman. If you will stop there until to-morrow, this young man and I will scour the country round about, and try to find some news of your Prince. The young man will return and report to you to-morrow morning. And if you should need help, or escort, he will aid and obey you as your servant. As for me, unless we have found the Prince, I shall continue searching for him. There is a prince in the city to the north of my master's tower, and it is not unlikely that it is he whom you seek."

"You can find out if it is he," answered the Princess, "by asking about the philopena."

"That will I do," said the Gryphoness, "and I will return hither as speedily as possible." And, with a respectful salutation, the Gryphoness and the Absolute Fool departed by different ways.

The Princess then repaired to the inn, where she took lodgings.

The next morning, the Absolute Fool came back to the inn, and seeing the Princess, said: "I rode until after night-fall, searching for the Prince, before it occurred to me that, even if I should find him, I would not know him in the dark. As soon as I thought of that, I rode straight to the nearest house, and slept until daybreak, when I remembered that I was to report to you this morning. But as I have heard no news of the Prince, and as this is a beautiful, clear day, I think it would be extremely foolish to remain idly here, where there is nothing of interest going on, and when a single hour's delay may cause you to miss the object of your search. The Prince may be in one place this morning, and there is no knowing where he will be in the afternoon. While the Gryphoness is searching, we should search also. We can return before sunset, and we will leave word here as to the direction we have taken, so that when she returns, she can quickly overtake us. It is my opinion that not a moment should be lost. I will be your guide. I know this country well."

The Princess thought this sounded like good reasoning, and consented to set out. There were some beautiful mountains to the south-east; and among these, the Absolute Fool declared, a prince of good taste would be very apt to dwell. They, therefore, took this direction. But when they had travelled an hour or more, the mountains began to look bare and bleak, and the Absolute Fool declared that he did not believe any prince would live there. He therefore advised that they turn into a road that led to the north-east. It was a good road; and therefore he thought it led to a good place, where a person of good sense would be likely to reside. Along this road they therefore travelled. They had ridden but a few miles when they met three men, well armed and mounted.

These men drew up their horses, and respectfully saluted the Princess.

"High-born Lady," they said, "for by your aspect we know you to be such, we would inform you that we are the soldiers of the King, the outskirts of whose dominions you have reached. It is our duty to question all travellers, and, if their object in coming to our country is a good one, to give them whatever assistance and information they may require. Will you tell us why you are come?"

"Impertinent vassals!" cried the Absolute Fool, riding up in a great passion. "How dare you interfere with a princess who has left her city because it was so dull and stupid, and is endeavoring to find a prince, with whom she has eaten a philopena, in order that she may marry him. Out of my way, or I will draw my sword and cleave you to the earth, and thus punish your unwarrantable curiosity!"

The soldiers could not repress a smile.

"In order to prevent mischief," they said to the Absolute Fool, "we shall be obliged to take you into custody."

This they immediately did, and then requested the Princess to accompany them to the palace of their King, where she would receive hospitality and aid.

The King welcomed the Princess with great cordiality. He had no son, and he much wished he had one; for in that case it might be his Prince for whom the young lady was looking. But there was a prince, he said, who lived in a city to the north, who was probably the very man; and he would send and make inquiries. In the mean time, the Princess would be entertained by himself and his Queen; and, if her servant would make a suitable apology, his violent language would be pardoned. But the Absolute Fool positively refused to do this.

"I never apologize," he cried. "No man of spirit would do such a thing. What I say, I stand by."

"Very well," said the King; "then you shall fight a wild beast." And he gave orders that the affair should be arranged for the following day.

In a short time, however, some of his officers came to him and told him that there were no wild beasts; those on hand having been kept so long that they had become tame.

"To be sure, there's the old lion, Sardon," they said; "but he is so dreadfully cross and has had so much experience in these fights, that for a long time it has not been considered fair to allow any one to enter the ring with him."

"It is a pity," said the King, "to make the young man fight a tame beast; but, under the circumstances, the best thing to do will be to represent the case to him, just as it is. Tell him we are sorry we have not an ordinary wild beast; but that he can take his choice between a tame one and the lion Sardon, whose disposition and experience you will explain to him."

When the matter was stated to the Absolute Fool, he refused with great scorn to fight a tame beast.

"I will not be degraded in the eyes of the public," he said; "I will take the old lion."

The next day, the court and the public assembled to

see the fight; but the Queen and our Princess took a
ride into the country, not wishing to witness a combat
of this kind, especially one which was so unequal.
The King ordered that every advantage should be
given to the young man, in order that he might have
every possible chance of success in fighting an animal
which had been a victor on so many similar occasions.
A large iron cage, furnished with a turnstile, into
which the Absolute Fool could retire for rest and refreshment, but where the lion could not follow him,
was placed in the middle of the arena, and the youth
was supplied with all the weapons he desired. When
every thing was ready, the Absolute Fool took his
stand in the centre of the arena, and the door of the
lion's den was opened. The great beast came out, he
looked about for an instant, and then, with majestic
step, advanced toward the young man. When he was
within a few paces of him, he crouched for a spring.

The Absolute Fool had never seen so magnificent a
creature, and he could not restrain his admiration.
With folded arms and sparkling eyes, he gazed with
delight upon the lion's massive head, his long and
flowing mane, his magnificent muscles, and his powerful feet and legs. There was an air of grandeur and
strength about him which completely enraptured the
youth. Approaching the lion, he knelt before him,
and gazed with wondering ecstasy into his great, glow-
ing eyes. "What glorious orbs!" he inwardly exclaimed. "What unfathomable expression! What
possibilities! What reminiscences! And everywhere,
what majesty of curve!"

The lion was a good deal astonished at the conduct of the young man; and he soon began to suppose that this was not the person he was to fight, but probably a keeper, who was examining into his condition. After submitting to this scrutiny a few minutes, he gave a mighty yawn, which startled the spectators, but which delighted the Absolute Fool; for never before had he beheld such a depth of potentiality. He knelt in silent delight at this exhibition of the beauty of strength.

Old Sardon soon became tired of all this, however, and he turned and walked back to his den. "When their man is ready," he thought to himself, "I will come out and fight him."

One tremendous shout now arose from the multitude. "The youth has conquered!" they cried. "He has actually frightened the lion back into his den!" Rushing into the arena, they raised the Absolute Fool upon their shoulders and carried him in triumph to the open square in front of the palace, that he might be rewarded for his bravery. Here the King, followed by his court, quickly appeared; for he was as much delighted as any one at the victory of the young man.

"Noble youth," he exclaimed, "you are the bravest of the brave. You are the only man I know who is worthy of our royal daughter, and you shall marry her forthwith. Long since, I vowed that only with the bravest should she wed."

At this moment, the Queen and the Princess, returning from their ride, heard with joy the result of the combat; and riding up to the victor, the Queen declared that she would gladly join with her royal husband in giving their daughter to so brave a man.

The Absolute Fool stood for a moment in silent thought; then, addressing the King, he said:

" Was Your Majesty's father a king? "

" He was," was the answer.

" Was his father of royal blood? "

" No ; he was not," replied the King. "My grandfather was a man of the people ; but his pre-eminent virtue, his great ability as a statesman, and the dignity and nobility of his character made him the unanimous choice of the nation as its sovereign."

" I am sorry to hear that," said the Absolute Fool ; " for it makes it necessary for me to decline the kind offer of your daughter in marriage. If I marry a princess at all, she must be one who can trace back her lineage through a long line of royal ancestors." And as he spoke, his breast swelled with manly pride.

For a moment, the King was dumb with rage. Then loudly he shouted: " Ho, guards! Annihilate him! Avenge this insult! "

At these words, the sword of every by-stander leaped from its scabbard; but, before any one could take a step forward, the Princess seized the Absolute Fool by his long and flowing locks, and put spurs to her horse. The young man yelled with pain, and shouted to her to let go ; but she held firmly to his hair, and as he was extraordinarily active and fleet of foot, he kept pace with the galloping horse. A great crowd of people started in pursuit, but as none of them were mounted, they were soon left behind.

" Let go my hair !   Let go my hair ! " shouted the
Absolute Fool, as he bounded along.   " You don't
know how it hurts.   Let go !   Let go ! "

But the Princess never relinquished her hold until
they were out of the King's domain.

" A little more," cried the indignant youth, when
she let him go, " and you would have pulled out a
handful of my hair."

" A little less," said the Princess, contemptuously,
" and you would have been cut to pieces ; for you
have not sense enough to take care of yourself.   I am
sorry I listened to you, and left the inn to which the
Gryphoness took me.   It would have been far better to
wait there for her as she told me to do."

" Yes," said the Absolute Fool ; " it would have
been much better."

" Now," said the Princess, " we will go back there,
and see if she has returned."

" If we can find it," said the other, " which I very
much doubt."

There were several roads at this point and, of
course, they took the wrong one.   As they went on,
the Absolute Fool complained bitterly that he had left
his horse behind him, and was obliged to walk.   Sometimes he stopped, and said he would go back after it ;
but this the Princess sternly forbade.

When the Gryphoness reached the city of the Prince,
it was night ; but she was not sorry for this.   She did
not like to show herself much in the daytime, because
so many people were frightened by her.   After a good

deal of trouble, she discovered that the Prince had
certainly left the city, although his guardians did not
seem to be aware of it. They were so busy with a
new palace, in part of which they were living, that
they could not be expected to keep a constant eye upon
him. In the morning, she met an old man who knew
her, and was not afraid of her, and who told her that
the day before, when he was up the river, he had seen
the Prince on his white horse, riding on the bank of
the stream ; and that near him, in the water, was something which now looked like a woman, and again like
a puff of mist. The Gryphoness reflected.

" If this Prince has gone off in that way," she said
to herself, " I believe that he is the very one whom
the Princess is looking for, and that he has set out in
search of her ; and that creature in the water must be
our Water Sprite, whom our master has probably sent
out to discover where the Prince is going. If he had
told me about this, it would have saved much trouble
From the direction in which they were going, I feel
sure that the Water Sprite was taking the Prince to
the Land of the Lovely Lakes. She never fails to go
there, if she can possibly get an excuse. I will follow
them. I suppose the Princess will be tired, waiting at
the inn ; but I must know where the Prince is, and if
he is really her Prince, before I go back to her."

When the Gryphoness reached the Land of the
Lovely Lakes, she wandered all that day and the next
night ; but she saw nothing of those for whom she was
looking.

The Princess and the Absolute Fool journeyed on until near the close of the afternoon, when the sky began to be overcast, and it looked like rain. They were then not far from a large piece of water; and at a little distance, they saw a ship moored near the shore.

" I shall seek shelter on board that ship," said the Princess.

" It is going to storm," remarked the Absolute Fool. " I should prefer to be on dry land."

" As the land is not likely to be very dry when it rains," said the Princess, " I prefer a shelter, even if it is upon wet water."

" Women will always have their own way," muttered the Absolute Fool.

The ship belonged to a crew of Amazon sailors, who gave the Princess a hearty welcome.

" You may go on board if you choose," said the Absolute Fool to the Princess, " but I shall not risk my life in a ship manned by women."

" It is well that you are of that opinion," said the Captain of the Amazons, who had heard this remark ; " for you would not be allowed to come on board if you wished to. But we will give you a tent to protect you and the horse in case it should rain, and will send you something to eat."

While the Princess was taking tea with the Amazon Captain, she told her about the Prince, and how she was trying to find him.

" Good ! " cried the Captain. " I will join in the search, and take you in my ship. Some of my crew told me that yesterday they saw a young man, who looked like a prince, riding along the shore of a lake which adjoins the one we are on. In the morning we will sail after him. We shall keep near the shore, and your servant can mount your horse and ride along the edge of the lake. From what I know of the speed of this vessel, I think he can easily keep up with us."

Early in the morning, the Amazon Captain called her crew together. " Hurrah, my brave girls ! " she said. " We have an object. I never sail without an object, and it lights me to get one. The purpose of our pres⁻nt cruise is to find the Prince of whom this Princess is in search ; and we must spare no pains to bring him to her, dead or alive."

Luckily for her peace of mind, the Princess did not hear this speech. The day was a fine one, and before long the sun became very hot. The ship was sailing quite near the land, when the Absolute Fool rode down to the water's edge, and called out that he had something very important to communicate to the Princess. As he was not allowed to come on board, she was obliged to go on shore, to which she was rowed in a small boat.

"I have been thinking," said the Absolute Fool, " that it is perfectly ridiculous, and very uncomfortable, to continue this search any longer. I would go back, but my master would not suffer me to return without knowing where you are going. I have, therefore, a plan to propose. Give up your useless search for this Prince, who is probably not nearly so handsome and intellectual as I am, and marry me. We will then return, and I will assume the reins of government in your domain.''

"Follow the vessel," said the Princess, " as you have been doing; for I wish some one to take care of my horse." And without another word, she returned to the ship.

" I should like to sail as far as possible from shore during the rest of the trip," said she to the Captain.

"Put the helm bias!" shouted the Amazon Captain to the steers-woman; " and keep him well out from land."

When they had sailed through a small stream into the lake adjoining, the out-look, who was swinging in a hammock hung between the tops of the two masts, sang out, " Prince ahead!" Instantly all was activity on board the vessel. Story books were tucked under coils of rope, hem stitching and embroidery were laid aside, and every woman was at her post.

" The Princess is taking a nap," said the Captain, " and we will not awaken her. It will be so nice to surprise her by bringing the Prince to her. We will run our vessel ashore, and then steal quietly upon him. But do not let him get away. Cut him down, if he resists!"

The Prince, who was plainly visible only a short distance ahead, was so pleasantly employed that he had not noticed the approach of the ship. He was sitting upon a low, moss-covered rock, close to the water's edge; and with a small hand-net, which he had found on the shore, he was scooping the most beautiful fishes from the lake, holding them up in the sunlight to ad-

mire their brilliant colors and graceful forms, and then
returning them uninjured to the water. The Water
Sprite was swimming near him, and calling to the fish
to come up and be caught; for the gentle Prince
would not hurt them. It was very delightful and rare
sport, and it is not surprising that it entirely engrossed
the attention of the Prince. The Amazons silently
landed, and softly stole along the shore, a little back
from the water. Then, at their Captain's command,
they rushed upon the Prince.

It was just about this time that the Gryphoness, who
had been searching for the Prince, caught her first
sight of him. Perceiving that he was about to be
attacked, she rushed to his aid. The Amazon sailors
reached him before she did, and seizing upon him they
began to pull him away. The Prince resisted stoutly;
but seeing that his assailants were women, he would
not draw his sword. The Amazon Captain and mate,
who were armed with broad knives, now raised their
weapons, and called upon the Prince to surrender or
die. But at this moment, the Gryphoness reached the
spot, and catching the Captain and mate, each by an
arm, she dragged them back from the Prince. The
other Amazons, however, continued the combat; and
the Prince defended himself by pushing them into the
shallow water, where the Water Sprite nearly stifled
them by throwing over them showers of spray. And
now came riding up the Absolute Fool. Seeing a
youth engaged in combat with the Amazon sailors, his
blood boiled with indignation.

" A man fighting women! " he exclaimed. " What

a coward! My arm shall ever assist the weaker sex.''

Jumping from the horse, he drew his sword, and rushed upon the Prince. The Gryphoness saw the danger of the latter, and she would have gone to his assistance, but she was afraid to loosen her hold of the Amazon Captain and mate.

Spreading her wings she flew to the top of a tree where she deposited the two warlike women upon a lofty branch, from which she knew it would take them a long time to get down to the ground. When she descended she found that the Absolute Fool had reached the Prince. The latter, being a brave fellow, although of so gentle a disposition, had been glad to find a man among his assailants, and had drawn his sword to defend himself. The two had just begun to fight when the Gryphoness seized the Absolute Fool by the waist and hurled him backward into some bushes.

'' You must not fight him ! '' she cried to the Prince. '' He is beneath your rank ! And as you will not draw your sword against these Amazons you must fly from them. If you run fast they cannot overtake you.''

The Prince followed her advice, and sheathing his sword he rapidly ran along the bank, followed by some of the Amazons who had succeeded in getting the water out of their eyes and mouths.

'' Run from women !'' contemptuously remarked the Absolute Fool. '' If you had not interfered with me,'' he said to the Gryphoness, '' I should soon have put an end to such a coward.''

The Prince had nearly reached the place opposite to

which the ship was moored, when the Princess, who
had been awakened by the noise of the combat, appeared upon the deck of the vessel. The moment she
saw the Prince, she felt convinced that he was certainly
the one for whom she was looking. Fearing that the
pursuing Amazons might kill him, she sprang from the
vessel to his assistance; but her foot caught in a rope,
and instead of reaching the shore, she fell into the
water, which was here quite deep, and immediately
sank out of sight. The Prince, who had noticed her
just as she sprang, and who felt equally convinced that
she was the one for whom he was searching, stopped
his flight and rushed to the edge of the bank. Just as
the Princess rose to the surface, he reached out his
hand to her, and she took it.

"Philopena!" cried the Prince.

"You have won," said the Princess, gayly shaking
the water from her curls, as he drew her ashore.

At the request of the Princess, the pursuing Amazons forbore to assail the Prince, and when the Captain and the Mate had descended from the tree, every
thing was explained.

Within an hour, the Prince and Princess, after taking kind leave of the Gryphoness, and Water Sprite,
and of the Amazon sailors, who cheered them loudly,
rode away to the city of the Princess; while the three
servants of the Inquisitive Dwarf returned to their
master to report what had happened.

The Absolute Fool was in a very bad humor; for he
was obliged to go back on foot, having left his horse in
the kingdom where he had so narrowly escaped being

killed; and, besides this, he had had his hair pulled;
and had not been treated with proper respect by either
the Princess or the Gryphoness. He felt himself
deeply injured. When he reached home, he determined that he would not remain in a position where his
great abilities were so little appreciated. " I will do
something," he said, " which shall prove to the world
that I deserve to stand among the truly great. I will
reform my fellow beings, and I will begin by reforming
the Inquisitive Dwarf." Thereupon he went to his
master, and said:

"Sir, it is foolish and absurd for you to be med-
dling thus with the affairs of your neighbors. Give up
your inquisitive habits, and learn some useful business.
While you are doing this, I will consent to manage
your affairs."

The Inquisitive Dwarf turned to him, and said: "I
have a great desire to know the exact appearance of
the North Pole. Go and discover it for me."

The Absolute Fool departed on this mission, and
has not yet returned.

When the Princess, with her Prince, reached her
city, her uncles were very much amazed; for they had
not known she had gone away. " If you are going to
get married," they said, " we are very glad; for then
you will not need our care, and we shall be free from
the great responsibility which is bearing us down."

In a short time the wedding took place, and then
the question arose in which city should the young
couple dwell. The Princess decided it.

" In the winter," she said to the Prince, " We will

live in your city, where all is life and activity; and where the houses are so well built with all the latest improvements. In the summer, we will come to my city, where every thing is old, and shady, and serene." This they did, and were very happy.

The Gryphoness would have been glad to go and live with the Princess, for she had taken a great fancy to her; but she did not think it worth her while to ask permission to do this.

" My impulses, I know, are good," she said; " but my appearance is against me."

As for the Water Sprite, she was in a truly disconsolate mood, because she had left so soon the Land of the Lovely Lakes, where she had been so happy. The more she thought about it, the more she grieved; and one morning, unable to bear her sorrow longer, she sprang into the great jet of the fountain. High into the bright air the fountain threw her, scattering her into a thousand drops of glittering water; but not one drop fell back into the basin. The great, warm sun drew them up; and, in a little white cloud, they floated away across the bright blue sky.